No.

MW00461435

Shantee' A. Parks

Barbara,
Thank you
For your
Support!
Happy reading!
Posey Parks

POSEY PARKS PUBLISHING

Girl *Power*

Copyright © 2015, 2016 by Shantee' A. Parks

Published by Posey Parks Publishing

www.poseyparkspublishing.com

All rights reserved.

∞

Acknowledgements

This book is dedicated to those who stand by me through it all.

Table of Contents

CHAPTER ONE

COLLEGE COMING TO A CLOSE

It's the last semester of school and boy am I glad to be graduating soon. All the studying for tests was becoming tiresome. I just needed a break. Actually a long break! I mean, if I have to pull another all-nighter again, I'm going to lose it. This is what I get for studying to be a doctor. Eight years of study. Shit, it hasn't been all bad. The parties, the girls! Did I mention the girls? Yeah that's the best part. I'm not your normal guy; I don't mind banging random college girls but after so long, I want to spoon a little and have a normal conversation, other than "what time are we hooking up?" Weird right? I mean, what guy wants to have a relationship.

My roommate has been with the same woman for the last two years. He said she's the one, and he wants to settle down with her. If you think about it, he probably did right, because he fucked as many bitches as he could before Melissa. Ryan and Melissa, oh it sounds perfect, as women love to say. Oh, how could I forget; my name is Brandon Christopher Asher II. I come from a long line of doctors. It's second nature that I would become a doctor, too. My dad didn't pressure me, he said I could be anything I wanted to be. I smile when I think of that talk I had with my Dad.

Family means everything to me. My parents, having been married for almost thirty years, and still go out on dates and take special vacations. I catch them sometimes when they don't know anyone is looking. My Dad would walk up behind my Mom, wrap his arms around her waist, kiss the back of her head, and tell her how much he loves her. My Mother would turn around in his arms, giving him a long kiss. If that's not love, I don't know what is. All my friends tell me I'm lucky because my parents are still married, let alone showing affection toward one another. If they got a divorce it would shatter me. However, I know I have to be a man and realize every relationship doesn't always work out. If they broke up, I would definitely ask why. I would want to learn from their mistakes.

∞

My Mom and Dad met shortly after my father became a doctor. He entered the deli to order his favorite pastrami sandwich. My father looked across the diner, and there saw the love of his life. She was sitting at the table with two friends. Her smile is what attracted him to her. He went over to introduce himself to the ladies.

"Hello my name is Brandon Asher. I was standing over at the counter when I noticed your smile." The women giggled.

"It's a pleasure to meet you," she said extending her hand. "I'm Susan Ruethers."

"I would love to call you sometime and possibly take you out to dinner," said Brandon.

"Sounds nice!" she smiled.

She gave him her phone number and the rest is history.

Back to my roommate. Ryan and I were roommates in the dorms, then I bought a condo and told him we could continue being roommates. On any given day when I get home, Ryan and Melissa are either cuddled up on the couch watching a movie, studying, playing board games; you get the gist. They are always together. They are not the only reason I want a girlfriend; I just want that special beautiful lady in my life. I sigh and sit here in the library counting down the days to graduation. The women I meet say I'm incapable of love. My friend Francesca said I'm too picky, and that I always, always find something wrong with a woman. I don't think that is true, but if you laugh like a fucking Hyena, I'm not listening to that shit for the next thirty years. Ok, it's usually two things that bug me about a woman before I bid her good riddance. I admit women are always willing to jump in my bed.

They say I have sexy brown and blonde hair. My hair is medium length, but curly. My eyes are grey, I have defined facial features, 6'3" tall, and defined abs is my other strong suit. I love to work out; I'm in the gym like 5 times a week. There are quite a few women wanting to be my girlfriend, but I'm not feeling any of them. Here comes a few of them now.

"Hi Brandon," they said in cadence as they wave and snicker as they walk by.

"Hi ladies."

Most of the women are pretty, but they are on that marriage train. They only want to get married, have kids, and live happily ever after. I know it's not that easy. I've observed my parent's marriage; they go on vacations together to keep it fresh. I don't want a woman who only wants to get married. She needs to have her own life. Fuck, want more for yourself than to sit around exchanging stories about wedding dresses and honeymoons. I looked down at my watch and noticed its five minutes to 10 a.m. I need to get across campus to my anatomy class. If I'm late, Professor Ross will embarrass me. I gather my books into my backpack as swiftly as I can and dart out of the library. I run clear across campus. I enter the lecture hall at exactly 10 a.m.

"Mr. Asher, you're late," she scoffed standing at the board writing down the assignment with her back to me.

"Professor Ross, I'm on time," I pleaded.

"Take your seat and tell me all the names of the different bones in the body."

Yep, she's tough.

After class, I head over to our Frat house to do an alcohol tally for the party Friday.

Man, have I fucked a lot of chicks in this house. I love fucking women and making them cum. One thing I don't do is eat a lot of pussy. That is something I will do for my woman when I have one. There are so many trifling chicks out there; they will ride my dick in the afternoon, then another dude's dick later that night. So I'm not putting my face near that kind of pussy.

"Hey Jas, what's up man?" I asked giving him a pound on his fist.

"Hey Brandon my man, you ready to party?" asked Jas.

"Shit yeah! I came over to see how much liquor we needed." I walked around to the back of the bar.

We have a little back door connection on our liquor and beer. We pay a set fee and the booze just falls off the truck into the trunk of my car. I smiled. After filling my liquor order, I went over to the hospital for my rotations. I never told my friends that I wanted the happily ever after life, because they would just torment me. Only Ryan and Stan know. Therefore, I played the single guy. I wanted it to happen naturally and believe me, I will know it when she comes along. I'm working in Pediatrics today. It's rewarding to take care of the kids, but I don't like to see the little ones sick. They should be outside playing or working their parent's nerves.

After work, I sometimes crave a late night snack so I head over to Emack & Bolio's Ice Cream Shop on Brookline Avenue. I entered the shop and waved at Fred who's helping another customer. I pulled out my cell phone to check my social media.

"I want to try something different. What do you suggest?" asked the woman.

"Pistachio is our number one flavor!" assured Fred.

"No that sounds gross. Let me try-,"

I looked up from my phone. "Miss, you are missing out, how about you try it? Just a sample?" I suggested.

"No thanks," the woman said.

Man is she beautiful. When she turned in my direction, I couldn't help but notice her beautiful brown eyes.

"I'll tell you what, if you don't like it you can chuck it." I don't wait for her to answer. Fred let me order a medium bowl of the pistachio.

"Sure buddy, coming right up."

I looked behind me and noticed the line was getting long, but I don't care. I took the bowl from Fred and spoon out a small amount and attempt to feed it to her.

"What are you doing?" she asked.

"Just take a bite. We are holding up the line. If you don't like it, I'll buy you whatever you want."

She looks at me with untrusting eyes and takes the spoon into her mouth. I watched her mouth slowly turn the ice cream around in her mouth and my dick got hard.

"It's ok," she said scrunching up her face.

"Alright give the lady whatever she wants," I said as I pulled out some cash to pay for our order.

"Thank you," she said.

"Will you sit with me for a bit, please?" I asked.

She hesitated, "Yeah."

I found us a table, placed our orders down, then pulled out a chair for her. I turned around to face the remaining customers.

"I apologized for the inconvenience."

She pulled me by my arm. "Sit down. You're being over dramatic."

"Yeah, sometimes I like to be the center of attention. By the way my name is Brandon. Your name?"

"Zoey, nice to meet you."

"The pleasure is all mine," I smiled.

I caught her blushing.

"So Brandon, do you do that for all the undecided customers? Feed them and buy them ice cream?"

"No Zoey just the pretty ones."

There's was an awkward silence.

"So Zoey, what's your favorite thing to do in the city?"

She smiled. "Ice skate."

"Brandon, what about you? No let me guess, Ice hockey!"

"Wow, that is stereotypical!"

She covered her mouth and laughed. "Ok what is it then?"

"No you guessed right." We both laughed loudly.

"So you don't want to get a new spoon? You don't know where my mouth has been."

All I could think about was how I wanted to get to know her mouth and more.

"I didn't think about it. Should I be worried? Do you have cooties?"

She covered her mouth and laughed again. I grabbed her hand and moved it from her mouth.

"Don't cover your mouth, you have a beautiful smile!"

She was quiet then said, "No, I don't have cooties. How often do you come here for ice cream?"

"A couple of times a week."

"Have you lived here all your life?" I asked.

"No, I'm from South Carolina. I'm here for school, but I had to drop out in my final year because I couldn't afford to pay. So right now I'm just working to save enough money to get back in next semester."

"What school did you attend?"

"Boston University."

"Are you in school?" she asked.

"Yes, I attend Harvard."

I didn't want to tell her my school because I didn't want to come off as privileged.

"That's cool!" she said with a big smile, this time not covering her mouth.

I couldn't help but to give a huge smile back. I hoped I had a piece of paper in my pocket. Normally I did, since I'm always taking notes. Yes! I found some paper, I'm in business, I thought.

"We are having a Fraternity party this Friday night. I would like you to come. Here's the name of the fraternity and the time it starts. Don't laugh but when you come, ask for B Dawg."

She looked over the note, "I will think about it."

"It was really nice to meet you," she said as she stood to her feet extending her hand for mine.

I took her hand in mine and kissed the back of it. I don't know why I did that; I had never done that before, but I needed to touch her skin in some way.

"Let me walk you out," I said releasing her hand.

"That's not necessary."

"I insist."

We strolled to the exit.

"Please, after you," I said.

I just had to let her walk in front so I could get a good picture of her ass.

Damn! Her ass was fat.

"I don't have a car, but please don't worry about me," she stated.

"I could drop you off wherever you need to go."

"No, I don't even know you!" she replied with raised eyebrows.

"Alright, well at least let me walk with you to the train or bus station?"

"Alright."

It was a beautiful spring night and I was walking with this beautiful woman. I would say my day was going pretty well. I hope I was not looking corny by smiling at her too much. Let me just tell you what this woman looked like. Her skin was a beautiful mocha color. It looked so smooth. She's got to be about 5'5, a petite frame with an ass that just won't quit. She's wearing a pink t-shirt, tight blue jeans, and a pair of navy gym shoes.

"How far do you live from here?" I just wanted to see her lips move because they were simply perfect. I could tell if I kissed her I wouldn't want to stop. Her eyes are a cute oval shape and her nose was the perfect size for her face. Her hair had these deep pretty black coils that looked like thick spirals, the kind you can't keep your hands out of. I kept asking her questions so I could hear her voice, and I loved to make her laugh. Did I tell you she was perfect? Perfect for me. Shoot, I forgot to ask her if she had a boyfriend.

"What will your boyfriend say about another man walking you safely to your destination?"

I ran my fingers through my curly locks awaiting her answer.

"I wouldn't know because I don't have a boyfriend."

I smiled at her, a little anxiously. I had to get my emotions under control.

"Can I see your cell?" I asked.

"Why?"

"So I can store my phone number in it."

She reluctantly passed me her phone. I typed in my entire name then took a photo of myself and stored it with my number. I handed her phone back and I removed mine from my jean's pocket.

"Can you stand right here against the building?"

I raised my cell phone getting ready to take the picture.

"What was your favorite teddy bear as a child?"

She laughed and I snapped the picture. She immediately grabbed my arm trying to see the picture.

I showed her and of course, she said, "Erase it."

"I will do no such thing. You look absolutely beautiful."

She stopped dead in her tracks. I turned around immediately and asked her, "What's wrong?" while I saved her picture.

"What are you doing?"

"Getting to know you, if you will let me," I said with a serious face.

She didn't say a word just continued walking by my side.

"Ok, I'm just about done, what is your last name?"

"Robinson."

I typed in her last name then returned my phone to my jean's back pocket.

"So, do you come from a large family?" I asked.

"I am an only child," replied Zoey.

"What about you?" she asked.

"I have a sister. My extended family is quite large, though. My sister is older than I am, and is truly the boss. We had so many arguments growing up it was pure hell," I said expressing the level of torment my sister gave me by throwing my fist into the air.

Zoey couldn't stop laughing. I know you're asking yourself what makes her different from the loads of other women I have been with. I can't really explain it, but she doesn't try to be something she's not. She's just being herself, at least that's what it seems like. We walked down the steps to the subway station. She swiped her card twice once for her and once for me. I stood with her while she awaited her train.

"So do you have a girlfriend?" she asked looking up at me.

"No. I have been in medical school so I didn't have time for a girlfriend. I also think it's because I never came across the right woman."

I turned to face her. I placed my hands on her face and leaned down placing my lips over hers drawing them into mine again and again. God it's even better than I thought. I pulled her lips into mine continuously. I don't want to stop but I also didn't want her thinking I'm an overbearing weirdo. I pulled her face back from mine just a bit so I could look into those beautiful brown eyes. "I really hope to see you this Friday."

She held on to my forearms while I still held her face in my hands. She held my gaze.

"Maybe," she whispered.

Her train arrived. We said our goodbyes and I waved at her until her train took off at the speed of light. I stood there for a minute absorbing what just happened before walking back down the street to my truck. I really hope she can fit into my life.

CHAPTER TWO

ZOEY

I sat on the train in utter amazement. I couldn't help but touch my lips, they still vibrated from his kiss. Where has this man been all my life? This could be just the perfect time. Of course, I'm going to that party. I loved talking to him. He makes me laugh, amongst other things. God, I feel so giddy right now, like a teenager. Soon as I get home, I'm going to look him up. The man is walking sex. I mean, shit, he was drop dead gorgeous. When he kissed my lips, my pussy got wet instantly. I quickly took out my phone to look at his handsome face again. I've never been with a white man before, but I am curious to see what it would be like. I haven't had the best of luck with men, period, so I don't bother with them. Men just tell you what you want to hear to get in your pants and once they get the ass, they're out. Well, at least that's been my experience. I wouldn't know what to do with a boyfriend. I mean no, really, I wouldn't know what to do.

My life has not been cookie cutter like his probably has. My father died when I was five. My mom had her share of boyfriends. They always looked at me as if they wanted to have sex with me. One night my mom's boyfriend spent the night. I remember it like it was yesterday, all the laughing, heavy panting, and raunchy words coming from the other side of my wall. The bed moved violently against the wall while I heard my mother scream. I was so scared, I got under the covers. I was eight at the time. She started yelling things like, "That's the way I like it baby, Give it to me just like that!" Then it was over. Silence. Later that night, the creak of my bedroom door woke me. I figured it was my mom; boy was I wrong, it was her boyfriend. I felt him pull back my covers.

I looked up at him. He put his finger to his lips.

"Shush girl, you better be quiet, or I will have to hurt your mama."

I didn't know what to do. He yanked my pajama pants and panties off. He was hovering over me and just as he was about to take his pants down I heard, "Click clack."

My mother stood behind him with her shotgun pointing at his back.

"If you don't get the fuck off my daughter so help me I will bust a cap in yo' ass so fast! Do you hear me? Nice and slow. Let's go!"

"Ella!"

"Don't Ella me you mother fucka, just get the fuck out of my house!"

His name was Steve and that man ran fast up out of there.

My Mom locked the door, put the rifle away, and started my bath water. She came back into the room and pulled me up into her arms, holding me so tight, apologizing repeatedly. My Mom didn't bring men to our house any longer. After that ordeal, I had a wonderful childhood. I was always at my grandmother's with my cousins playing; just having fun. My mom was a nurse, so she worked long hours all the time. When I was thirteen my mother sat me down to have a heart to heart talk.

"Baby, I know it's been hard on you since your dad died," said Ella.

I somberly dropped my head holding my fingers together in my lap. "Yes mom, I miss him every day. I always think how daddy never tried to hurt me in any way. He just loved me."

"I know baby that's what a good father does," she said hugging me.

"I've met someone. He and I have been dating for a year now. I didn't want to bring him around until I was sure he was the right one. I would like us all to go to dinner this evening. I would like you two to get acquainted. Do you think you can do that for me?"

I looked up into my mother's eyes and I could see the need in her eyes to have love from this new man. "Yes mom, I can do it!" I sighed.

"Thank you baby," said Ella.

Later that evening my mother and I waited for Martin to arrive at the upscale restaurant.

My mother and I sat patiently in the lobby. I kept myself entertained by listening to my favorite songs on my IPod.

The waitress walked over to us. "Excuse me, Mrs. Robinson, Mr. Collier called. He asked me to seat you both. He said he will arrive shortly," said the waitress.

About fifteen minutes later a man approached our table standing next to my mother.

He greeted my mother by giving her a hug. "Ella, sorry I'm late."

He then walked over to me. "You must be Zoey," he said reaching out to shake my hand.

I removed my headphones and shook his hand. "My name is Martin Collier, nice to finally meet you. I've heard nothing but great things about you," he raved taking his seat next to my mother.

"I understand you're very active in sports, while still getting all A's. That is quite impressive."

Dinner went well. I talked more than I planned to. He seemed genuinely interested in me.

In the months to come, I got a chance to know Martin. I finally gave my Mom my blessing.

I told my Mom I thought it would be cool to have Martin around. After that conversation, everything moved quickly. There was a huge wedding. We had a special adoption ceremony within the wedding. Martin respected my decision not to want to change my last name out of respect for my dad. It was the happiest I'd been in years. I had a family again. He reminded me of my dad in many ways.

Martin always made sure I got to all my practices on time. He even waited until cheer practice was over, he didn't just drop me off. My mom rarely took me to practices due to her work schedule. He catered to my mother, always rubbing her feet when she got off work. He took care of us both. We did what any family did; we had family game night, special family dinners and vacations. Martin spoiled my mother to no end, buying her new trucks and jewelry. He was always kissing her, I thought it was so cute. Her friends would always tell her how fine her husband was and how lucky she was to have a man who loved her.

Martin had a fancy job. He was a young hotshot lawyer. He was 33 years old. My mother was just a couple years older than him. They were such a pretty couple, at least to me anyway. Nevertheless, no matter what, he was at my gymnast events, cheer competitions, and soccer games. Did I tell you we moved into this huge, fabulous house way out in the suburbs? I had everything a teenager could want and of course, at the age of fourteen I wanted everything! Boys were beginning to look at me because my breasts started growing out and my butt was getting bigger. I soon had my first little boyfriend who would ride with us to my cheer competitions. Martin would always give him a dirty look through the rearview mirror. He eventually stopped coming around. I later expressed my feelings to Martin.

"Zoey, boys only want one thing and you are not to give up your fruit to these nappy headed little boys. Do I make myself clear!?" He scolded me with a scowl on his face.

"Yes Martin, I understand."

"Good," he replied giving me a long hug.

When he released me from his arms, my eyes dropped down to his crotch and I noticed his penis was hard. I didn't react.

"I have homework to do," I stated.

I didn't understand why that happened. I soon got over that incident when he allowed my friends to sleep over that weekend. We had a ball. I told Martin that he was the best Father ever. I smiled at the thought of just being a kid. It was a long time before we were in close proximity again.

∞

One night my mom was working overnight. I was on the couch watching a scary movie sitting around as I always did. I was wearing what I always wore, a t-shirt, and shorts. I held the pillow tightly anticipating the scary scenes. Martin sat down next to me. He and I often watched movies together so I thought nothing of it. I put the pillow up to my face when the scary parts of the movie appeared.

"Hey, can I ask you a question?" Martin asked.

"Yeah," I said.

"Do you like the way you and your mother live?"

"Yes," I replied.

"Do you like seeing your mother happy?"

"Yeah, I love seeing the smile on her face every day!

I wouldn't change that for the world," I recited with excitement.

"I can keep her happy, but you have to promise to do something for me."

"Ok what's that?" I asked.

"If you say no, I will have to take all of your mother's toys away and yours, too. Do you understand?"

I swallowed hard, "What are you asking me?"

"I need you to make me happy if you want me to continue to make your mother happy."

"Make you happy how?" I asked in a low confused voice.

"Remember, if you say no I will take all your teenage goodies away and you won't get the new truck I planned to get for you next year."

He put his arm around my shoulders and got closer to my ear.

"I waited until you turned fifteen because I wanted you to be closer to the age of a woman."

"But I'm still a kid," I sadly replied with tears now starting to fall from my eyes.

"No baby, not with a body like yours," he replied greedily rubbing my leg.

He started kissing my neck and I felt disgusted. I didn't know what to do. He got on his knees in front of me and pulled off my shorts and panties. He spread my legs apart and pulled my sex close to his face. He licked between my legs in a slow steady motion. I didn't know how to feel at first, but it felt so good. My body started to come alive in ways I didn't know it could. I bucked my sex against his face as I closed my eyes and gripped the couch cushions tight.

"Please stop, something's not right, I'm about to pee on myself," I yelled as I squirmed.

He looked up at me. "It's alright, calm down. You have to let go. Let it happen, I promise it will be ok."

"He licked on my knob repeatedly. A feeling came over me that was indescribable. It felt so good when all my juices poured out of me into his mouth. He drank all of me.

"You taste so good I don't think I could ever let you go," he said lustfully.

I was terrified at that moment.

"Why do you want me and not my mother?"

He placed his hand on my face and said, "Because you're special."

In one fell swoop, he picked me up into his arms and carried me upstairs to my bedroom.

He kept telling me I was his princess and that I was made for him. He laid me down and started to remove his clothes until he was completely naked. I laid there in horror. He was about to take my virginity.

"The first time your mother showed me your picture I knew you were the one. My princess. I promise to give you the world as long as you behave."

"Are we clear?" he asked as he sat on his knees at my feet.

I nodded my head yes as the tears poured from my eyes. He did unspeakable things to me. He took me from childhood to womanhood in an instant.

CHAPTER THREE

ZOEY

A week later, Martin picked me up from school in the middle of the day. "I made you a doctor's appointment. My friend who is a doctor is going to prescribe you birth control pills. The doctor will explain how the pills work," Martin stated.

"You will need to take the pills everyday so that you don't get pregnant."

I cringed inside at his words.

"I will set an alarm on your cell phone to remind you to take the pill every day. Do you understand?" he asked in an even tone.

"Yes," I responded watching the trees go by as we drove home.

As time passed, I grew accustomed to doing sexual things exactly the way Martin wanted me to. I know it was sick, but I began to like it; a lot. What did I know? He stole my virginity and my innocence. I fell in love with him. Shit just thinking back on it fills me with anger. I want to kill him. He destroyed me for any man to come in my future. Every time I thought of what it would be like to have a boyfriend, I threw it out of my head because I knew that wasn't possible.

I stood looking at my reflection in my bathroom mirror sadly thinking how I could never have my own family or happiness.

"God, why would you let this happen to me?" I screamed as I fell to the floor. I curled up in a little ball holding myself tight. I'm so tired of not having a normal life. Well, let me get back to the story.

He treated me like a princess and told me he loved me every chance he got. He said he couldn't stop having sex with my mother for fear of her suspecting something was wrong.

One evening, I was doing my homework at the kitchen counter. Martin walked in and proceeded over to my mother, smacked her ass, then whispered something in her ear. I was furious. I pushed the bowl of fruit off the counter watching it shatter all over the floor. They turned and looked at me.

"What the hell is going on with you lately?" my mother asked sternly.

I stood there with my arms folded. I cut my eyes in Martin's direction and scurried from the kitchen.

"Get back here young lady!" my mother yelled.

I stood outside the kitchen while my mother continued to yell for my return.

"Don't worry about it Ella. I'll clean it up. She's just being a teenager, acting out."

"You are right," she replied in a tender voice.

"Thanks baby, I don't know what I would do if you didn't come into our lives!" she cooed kissing his cheek. I peeked around the corner watching them.

∞

Later that night after pleasing my mother, he came down to my bedroom. He quietly opened and closed my door then sat at my bedside.

"Zoey why are you acting like a child?" he asked angrily.

"Because I am a child," I commented with great anger.

"You are pleasing her like you do me and I don't like it one bit!" I pouted.

"I promise you that is far from the truth. You are the only one I wish to please!" Martin said.

"Then prove it," I said pulling my nightgown over my head and standing in front of him completely naked bringing him to his knees.

He tried to touch me. "No," I spat out pushing his hand away.

"You need to purchase my truck sooner than later. I want my Mazda truck next week before our weekend getaway or I will go stay at my grandmother's that weekend."

I stood there with my arms folded giving him a hard stare.

"Shit! Yes of course!" he grunted and groaned.

"Good! Now, I have to get some rest, I have school in the morning. Close my door on your way out," I commanded as I pulled my covers over my head.

I got my truck early just as I asked. I knew then I could get away with anything.

I was in love with my new truck, it came equipped with leather. All my friends were envious. My mother didn't understand why he bought me such an expensive truck. I didn't care how he explained his way out of it.

We had a huge Christmas party at our house that year. All of our family and friends attended. We had a ball.

My best friend Maya and I were online when we saw our favorite group was going to be in town. We didn't just want tickets we wanted front row tickets and backstage passes. I knew just how to get them. *I will offer good old Martin a blow job*, I thought as I smiled to myself. Maya and I looked into each other eyes and we both burst out laughing because we knew we had the same thought.

Maya had a soft pale complexion, long blonde hair, radiant blue eyes, and a petite frame.

I thought back to an earlier time when Maya and I were walking toward the soccer field for practice.

"Can you keep a secret? Listen, please don't say yeah and not mean it," asked Maya.

"Maya you're my best friend!" I confirmed stopping our stride. Maya turned and looked at me. "Maya we've been keeping each other's secrets since we were fourteen. And in that time have I told anyone anything?" I asked angrily with my hand on my hip.

"No you haven't," she affirmed.

"Fine," she said in an irritated tone.

"My stepfather makes me have sex with him."

My eyes bulged out of my head. "What! How long?"

"Shortly after I turned fifteen," she confirmed.

"Shit! Me too!" I admitted surprisingly.

"Our stepfathers work together right?" I asked.

"Yes. Maya I can't believe we are both going through the same thing."

"When I don't want to be bothered, I sometimes don't take a bath. Then he's uninterested."

"Zoey, it won't work, he makes me take a bath."

"Girl, once I learned what an orgasm was, I made sure I always get one. I sit on his face and ride it and I don't let him come up for air. I mean, shit, he's going to get off regardless," I protested.

I punched Maya's arm. "I still can't believe you Maya! How could you hold this in for so long? A whole year?"

"Sorry girl. I just didn't know how you would take it."

"It's cool, we are sisters forever. We'll get through this!" I said throwing my arm around her shoulder as we continued onto practice.

Back to the party. Maya and I walked around the party trying to find Martin. We spotted him talking to some of his colleagues. We decided to sit on the couch across the room from him so he could see us. Even though the room was crowded, everyone was so caught up in their own conversations, they didn't pay us any attention. I waited until we made eye contact. I stuck my tongue over to my right cheek and placed my hand up near my face. I motioned my fist back forth toward my jaw as my tongue pushed my inner cheek out a few times. It was priceless to watch how his eyes got as large as saucers. Maya got it all on video. Maya and I laughed out loud rocking back and forth on the couch in amusement.

CHAPTER FOUR

ZOEY

I lay here in my bed tonight thinking about what could be with this playboy model who claimed to be a doctor. He just met me and he kissed me. What's up with that? I touched my lips just thinking about the kiss we shared.

I've been with two other guys since my stepfather sexually molested me. I waited to be with another man until I was away at college. Rick was the first guy I was with intimately. He wasn't shit. That's why it was so fitting that his name rhymed with dick. I met him at a fraternity party. We hung out at my dorm a few times just talking and watching TV. Then one thing led to another and we were in my bed having sex. His dick was bigger than Martin's. He had a longer shaped penis. I remembered how it hurt and how sex hadn't hurt for me in the past because I had always cum a few times before fucking. His idea of foreplay was kissing my neck, rubbing on my breasts, then trying to stick his dick inside of me. I wanted to tell him to get the fuck off me. Instead, I made him sit up and watch me masturbate so we could have sex. I instructed him to put on the condom. I then pulled him over me, looked into his eyes, and took his lips within mine. He grabbed my hips and slammed inside me until I screamed. I hit him on his shoulder.

"What the fuck, that's not how you have sex," I affirmed.

"What?" he asked looking at me perplexed.

I took control by grabbing his ass with both hands and pushing him inside me slower. Telling him to move in a circular motion then to grab my leg and place it on his shoulder. Needless to say I didn't enjoy shit! No orgasm! You know what? I never had sex with him again. Every time I saw him around campus, we avoided each other like the plague.

My next sex buddy was Aaron. I had seen him around campus a few times but didn't think anything of it. One afternoon I was eating lunch in the cafeteria when he walked over to where I was sitting.

"Excuse me is anyone sitting here?" asked the young man.

I finished swallowing my soup and responded, "No."

"Cool," he said as he sat down.

I stared at him for a long time while I drank my grape juice. "You asked me if anyone was sitting here; you didn't ask if you could sit down."

He laughed. "Girl why are you playing hard to get?"

I set my juice bottle down on the table. "I'm not playyyinnng hard to get," I stressed.

"Oh so you're just stuck up?" he asked.

"No, I just don't have time for bullshit."

He smiled in a cocky manner. "Ok, I'll play."

"I'm not playing. I'm here to learn. I don't have time for a man."

"Listen, how about we just get to know each other. Let me take you out on a date, if you don't like me you don't have to see me again. Is that a deal?"

I pondered the idea for a minute while I looked over his handsome face. "Sure why not."

"Good."

We continued to eat our lunch and talk about our classes.

That Friday night I got ready for our date. I wore a cute little purple dress that stopped at my knees and some short black boots. I put a pack of condoms into my purse; made sure my short hair was cute and waited for my date.

Soon there was a knock at the door.

I opened my door and there was fine ass Aaron. He was about 5'10, milk chocolate skin, jet black hair cut low, brown eyes and a gorgeous smile. I'm sure that smile got him into so many girls' panties. I sure wanted to take him for a test drive, but first we would go to dinner.

He walked through the threshold of my dorm room leaving the door open. "Are you ready?"

"Yes Aaron, let me just grab a sweater."

We arrived at a popular pizza parlor for dinner.

After we ordered our food, we talked.

"Aaron where are you from?" I asked with a smile.

"Wow, I think that's the first time I've seen a smile on that beautiful face."

"So you've been watching me?" I grinned.

"Guilty. It's just hard to approach a woman who appears stand-offish."

"I will toast to that!" I said raising my mug filled with root beer.

He flashed his gorgeous smile and tapped his glass against mine.

"I am from South Carolina," I replied.

"Do you miss home?"

"Sometimes," I replied with sad eyes looking down at my drink.

"You never answered me. Where are you from?"

"Colorado."

"Damn you traded in one cold state for another!" we laughed.

"I know, but there are some really good companies to work for here."

After dinner, we went to play miniature golf; which was a lot of fun. It was the most fun I had in a long time. It was nice to just be a young person and not think about my past. Just live in the moment.

He walked me to my dorm door after our date.

"I had a nice time," I said with my back to my door as I looked into his eyes.

"So does that mean I can see you again?" he asked.

I smiled, "Yes."

I pulled him closer to me by his jacket until our lips touched. He held me by my waist as our tongues did an entangled dance. The kiss was so good I turned my doorknob with one hand behind my back pulling him into my room.

I released his lips long enough to put my privacy sign on the outside of my doorknob. I walked toward him until his legs were flush against my mattress.

Nervously he asked me, "Is your roommate coming back anytime soon?"

"It doesn't matter if she does, she knows not to enter," I said unbuttoning my dress down the front, pulling it over my head and throwing it to the floor.

His eyes roamed over my body landing on my ass covered in red satin panties then up into my eyes. "Damn your ass is fat!"

I laughed, then walked over to my purse to retrieve a condom. I walked back over to my bed standing before him. He pulled me by my ass, slid his hands down to my thighs sitting me in his lap. Our lips devoured each other's. I couldn't get enough of his kiss. Our sexual chemistry was obvious. I could tell just by the way we kissed that he would be a little more willing to cater to my needs. I helped him take off his clothes then slid the condom down his impressive sized dick. I moved up to the head of my bed; he followed. He again grabbed my ass this time pulling me underneath him. I wasn't wearing a bra so all he had to remove were my panties. He sucked on my nipples one by one. I exhaled as he moved down to my treasure box to retrieve his prize. He licked my clit in a circular motion driving me crazy. My eyes rolled to the back of my head. I held his head in place while I began to buck against his face wildly.

"Oh shit I'm cumming," I moaned. I held on tight while he drank all of me.

"That was nice," I breathed. He hovered over me, then leaned down kissing my lips. This was the first time I ever tasted myself. I was pleased with the way I tasted and pushed my tongue into his mouth, so I could taste all of me. He pushed inside me fast in that moment. I gasped then I quickly adjusted taking all of him inside me.

"Zoey you feel so good, shit!" he moaned in my ear as I wrapped my arms around his neck tightly. His pace increased with every stroke. I moved my hips in a circular motion sending him over the edge. That one move was all it took. He stroked in and out as his breathing intensified.

"Shit baby this is some good gooood pussy!" he groaned as he came.

He flopped down on top of me while his chest heaved in and out. I pushed him over on his back next to me.

"What the fuck was that!" I asked enraged while looking up at the ceiling then over at him.

He tried to cuddle with me but I pushed him away. I sat there pissed.

"Baby what do you want me to say? I ain't never had pussy that good! Look, how about you give me a chance to redeem myself. I promise not to cum quick this time."

I sat there in silence for a moment. "Alright."

I pulled the used condom off his dick, jumped off the bed, threw it in the trash, and retrieved another condom from my purse. I straddled his thighs and rolled the condom down his dick. I stroked his manhood up and down before easing my wet pussy down then up his dick repeatedly. I held onto his arms as I continued to push myself up and down. Just as it was starting to feel good to me, I saw that 'I'm about to cum face' and I stopped. I grabbed him by his balls and squeezed while I looked into his eyes. "You better not cum quick again," I threatened.

"Alright, alright, shit, I won't," he said with conviction.

I started to move myself up and down on his dick again. I threw my head back just as I was about to cum. He grabbed my hips, slammed into me and came. I was so pissed I wanted to kick him out.

I looked down at him with angry eyes. "Fuck that! You have to pay for that shit! You need to eat my pussy again!" I yelled.

He obliged and did a pretty good job at making me cum. I decided that was all he was good at. I fucked him a few more times so I could get him to lick my kitty cat.

I stand here at work serving drinks thinking back on my fucked up sex life.

"Hey Zoey can you run and grab a case of beer?" asked my coworker Felicia.

"Sure." I replied.

I made up my mind to go to the party Brandon invited me to. I won't have sex with him. I will just enjoy the free booze and great dancing, with a couple of my girls.

CHAPTER FIVE

FRAT PARTY

BRANDON

I stocked the bar and placed all the kegs strategically around the Frat house. These past few days had been hell. I couldn't get Zoey out of my head. I kept thinking about her beautiful brown face. When she turned and faced me in line at the ice cream parlor, her beauty instantly mesmerized me. I stand here in the hall for a moment due to the mountain of nerves overtaking me. I needed to lean against the wall for just a minute. I had to get a hold of my feelings. I adjusted my dick every time I thought about her big fat juicy ass.

Why did I kiss her? I asked myself as I ran my hand through my curly hair. Shit, I literally tried to fuck her out of my brain. Yup, that means I fucked as many girls as I could in a three-day period, and none of them fucking did it for me. I usually stuck to my plan. Only have sex with one woman a month. I just didn't have the time or energy to fuck several women daily. I worked rounds at the hospital and had to focus on school.

Right now, I was supposed to only be having sex with Sandy. I had been seeing her for two months instead of the one. I just kind of got lazy. I always kept Mindy around because I loved having sex with her. I also had sex with Nina and Trish. I had a bedroom here that I used just for sex. Let me see, so I had sex with Sandy and Mindy on the first day, Mindy and Nina the next, then Trish and Sandy yesterday. I took a break today. It all started Tuesday when I saw Mindy in the Library, as I thought back.

"Hey Mindy what's up?" I asked sitting down at the table next to her.

"Nothing much," she replied.

"Mindy do you have time to hook up this afternoon?"

"Yeah sure," Mindy smirked.

"I'll meet you at the frat house in an hour," she said.

"Cool I'll see you then," I confirmed.

I was lying on the bed with my eyes closed thinking about how I needed to kiss Zoey's soft lips again.

I must have been in deep thought because I didn't realize Mindy was standing there.

Mindy was a very pretty woman. She was 5'10, with the body of a track star, pale smooth skin, long brown hair, and beautiful green eyes. I liked messing around with Mindy because she doesn't want anything other than sex from me.

I sat straight up. "Sorry Mindy, I've been kind of distracted ever since I met this woman yesterday. I can't seem to get her off my mind. I need you to help me forget about her," I said rubbing her thighs.

Mindy looked down at me with a big smile. "I can absolutely help you!"

Mindy pulled my t-shirt over my head then removed her t-shirt throwing them to the floor.

"Brandon I must say, this is odd for you. You're not the kind of guy that thinks about a woman other than for sex," she affirmed as she stripped down naked.

"I know but she's different and I want to see her again," I admitted removing the condom from my jean pocket setting it next to me on the bed. I removed my shoes, jeans, then boxers.

"Mindy, I get the feeling that if she didn't see me again it wouldn't be a big deal. I don't know. I will probably never see her again, so I really don't want to talk about her," I said rolling the condom down on my dick.

"Fine not a problem. Let's just get to it then," she said leaning into my lips with a hard kiss.

I massaged her breasts while she straddled me with our lips still connected. I threw Mindy down on the bed, sat up between her legs, rubbing her pussy with one hand while stroking my dick in the other. I massaged her clit in a circular motion sending her to the brink.

"That's my girl, cum for Daddy."

I slid my dick up and down the slit of her wet pussy. Her green eyes begged me to make her cum again.

"Don't worry I'm about to give it to you," I confirmed sliding in with ease. "Yeah that's it, give me that pussy," I whispered in her ear.

I thrust in and out of her faster and faster. I could feel her walls closing in around my dick. She was about to cum. I stopped, sat up on my knees, and looked down at her. "Not yet." I pulled out of her, flipped her on her stomach, pulled her ass up, and slammed into her pussy. She screamed out. "Shit! Fuck me hard. Give it to me!" she demanded as I held onto her hips slamming into her repeatedly.

I knew I could depend on Mindy to keep the Zoey thoughts at bay. I was always careful to never tell a woman how good her pussy was. I never wanted her holding that over my head. Mindy had good pussy, but deep down I think she knew because out of all the women I've been with, she was the one I've been fucking the longest. If Mindy had feelings for me, she never told me. I asked her one time after sex if she wanted more. She told me no and I was good with that. I continued to pound away inside her until I finally came. I fell down beside Mindy out of breath.

"Are you good?" she asked.

"Yeah, you were just what the doctor ordered," I joked. We both laughed.

Ten minutes after Mindy left I was replaying that moment in time in my head when I kissed Zoey. "Shit, I've got it bad!"

Now back to the present day. I stood here obsessing over Zoey with feelings I've never had before. Why didn't I ever take the time to really get to know some of the women I slept with? I could have taken one of the ladies out to lunch. I know why. I just never had the desire to. Maybe they were not the type that I needed for my soul. I've never been with a black woman. I always found them beautiful but it was different when I met Zoey. She made my heart skip a beat. I had to get to know her. The feelings I had for Zoey were strong and too fast. I don't do feelings. I know, I know, I said I wanted a relationship. I think I've been alone for so long I wouldn't even know how to be in a relationship. It doesn't matter, she probably won't show tonight anyway. *There will be plenty of other chicks here for me tonight*," I thought.

I made my way down to the front door.

"Hey Gus, my man!" I said slapping him on the back.

"What's up bro?"

I pulled my cell phone from my pocket and showed him Zoey's picture.

"Do me a solid. If this woman shows up tonight text me."

"Sure thing man. Shit, she's pretty hot!" said Gus.

"Yeah, well I'm not sharing she's mine!" I confirmed.

"Hey man you know my motto: Bro's before hoes!"

I shot him a serious look.

"Sorry Brandon just kidding! Fuck, get a grip."

I've been serving up drinks for a couple hours and still no Zoey. I thought talking to people while I made drinks would keep my mind off of her. Shit, this was not working! Fuck, I needed to get her off my mind. I saw Mindy walking in my direction.

"Mindy! What would you like to drink?"

"Hi Brandon, I'll have a Bud Light," she said looking into my eyes and licking her lips.

As we stood there, eyes locked, I felt someone walk up.

"Hey Bartender, I will have a Tequila for me and two Whiskey sours for my friends."

My eyes left Mindy's and looked toward the direction of the voice. And there she was, Zoey. I half smiled at her.

"Coming right up! I'm happy you came Zoey."

Shit, I spilled one of the drinks.

"Oh shit, what's this Dr. Asher? All thumbs," teased Mindy as she walked over to Zoey.

"Damn girl, you must have gold between your legs to make Brandon Asher II nervous," she said close to Zoey's ear.

Mindy looked up at me. "See you around B Dawg!"

"You need to keep that one in check," spewed Zoey picking up the drinks as she walked off.

Great! For once can I focus on one woman?

CHAPTER SIX

BRANDON

"Hey Rob can you handle the bar by yourself for a while?"

"Yeah, I got it."

"Thanks," I replied as I grabbed a beer.

I walked around the house looking for Zoey trying not to look too excited.

Great, there she was dancing with her friends. I couldn't help but smile. Damn she was beautiful. I stood there, leaning against the wall across the room drinking my beer, watching her.

How I longed to taste her lips again. I made my way over to her on the dance floor.

I leaned down and whispered in Zoey's ear, "Thank you for coming tonight."

Her hair smelled like roses. She was wearing a skin tight short strappy black dress.

"You're welcome," she smiled up at me.

"You changed your hair."

"Yeah, women do that you know. Hey, meet my friends. Stacey, Tamika, this is Brandon."

"Nice to meet you both," I said shaking their hands.

"Hi Brandon," they both sang.

"Zoe, he's cute!" they cooed.

Zoey just smiled.

"Do you mind if I steal your friend for a little while ladies?" I asked looking into their pretty brown faces.

"Sure, go ahead, we are going to mingle a bit," said Stacey winking then taking Tamika's hand leading her through the crowd.

A slow song came on. "Dance with me Zoey." I didn't give her a chance to think about it, I just wrapped her arms around my neck.

I pulled her closer so she should could feel how much I missed her. She pulled back from me with a smile.

"Oh, you really have been thinking about me, I'm impressed. It seems you want more than just to see me," she teased.

"I do, but I would like to get to know you better first."

"Hmm that's odd, I didn't get the feeling you got to know a woman first before you fucked them."

I smiled down at her. "You're right, I don't."

A new song came on with a fast beat.

I ran my hand along her cheek as I leaned down to kiss her lips.

It was as if time stood still. I didn't care who saw us. I just knew in that moment I had to taste her.

"I've waited days to do that," I said in between a string of long kisses.

"Hey B Dawg, Rob needs your help!" Ted pleaded.

"Zoey, I need to help Rob. How about you find your friends, I will catch up soon."

"Ok," she stated.

As I walked away from her, I noticed all eyes were upon us. All because I chose to express the way, I felt for her. Well, they had better get used to it, because as long as Zoey was in the picture there would be plenty more of that to come.

I sprinted over to the bar. Hey man what happened?" I asked with my hands thrown up in the air.

"I was trying to open the keg and got backed up."

I walked over to the keg and opened it.

"Shit man, I am sorry, I never opened one before," Rob responded worriedly.

"It's cool man," I said grabbing his shoulder.

"Let's catch up these drink orders," I said.

"Hey Brandon, I ran into your girlfriend. She's throwing them back in the kitchen. Man that girl can drink," said Sheena.

I passed her a beer. "She's not my girlfriend, but she is someone I'm interested in."

"Wow, looks like hell has officially frozen over."

"Good one Sheena."

"Hey Jeff," I said motioning him to come over to the bar.

"Dude can you cover me? A friend of mine is here and I need to check on her."

"Oh yeah man, I never stand in the way of another man getting pussy," Jeff replied hitting me on the back.

"Thanks Jeff."

I made my way toward the kitchen. It was almost impossible to get through the crowd. I didn't have time to explain to Jeff it wasn't like that or to Sheena that I wanted Zoey to be my girlfriend. I entered the kitchen only to see Zoey in a drink competition with Allen.

"Alright, shows over!" I shouted as I took the cup out of Zoey's hand drinking it down myself.

"Hey, that was mine," she slurred grabbing up at my arms to get the cup back.

"Sorry baby, while you're here with me, I won't let anything happen to you. Old Allen here is our Frat drinking champion. I'm sure he failed to mention that. He loves making wagers against those who haven't been here before." I pulled Zoey into my arms and kissed her forehead. I looked over at her friends who were being entertained by a couple of guys. I made Zoey drink a couple of cups of water.

"Brandon that's enough; I don't want to drink anymore water."

"Zoey when was the last time you ate?"

"Around 3 p.m.," she confirmed.

"Listen I need you to drink one more cup of water and eat something. Doctor's orders!" I said looking down at my watch.

"I will let you have another drink in about an hour."

I noticed a handful of the women I had slept with were right there in the room. I better get Zoey out of here before someone made a scene. I ran over to the other side of the counter to make her a plate. I grabbed her a hamburger and added a salad w/ranch dressing to the plate. *With a body like hers, she's probably on a diet*, I thought. I picked up a bunch of napkins and motioned with my head for Zoey to follow me. I got her alone in one of the bedrooms upstairs. I made sure it wasn't my sex room. I quickly closed the door behind us and set her food down on the table so she could eat. I sat on the dresser across the room from her. I tried not to watch her eat but I just couldn't help it.

"Brandon, can you stop watching me eat?"

"Sorry- I didn't- mean to," I said stumbling over my words.

I never trip all over myself! What the fuck is going on?! I retrieved my cell phone from my pocket and looked down at it to keep me distracted.

"Brandon, you're so worried about me eating when was the last time you ate?"

"Zoey don't worry about it."

It was too late. She's now standing in front of me forcing her burger into my mouth. I watched her face while I chewed slowly.

"Oh shoot you got a little ketchup on your lip," she smirked.

"Let me grab a napkin," I replied.

"No I got it," she said licking it off my lips.

She stepped back and looked into my eyes. I lunged into her lips pulling up her dress at the same time as I sat her on my lap. I moaned her name against her lips.

"Zoey."

"Looks like someone wants to fuck me pretty bad," she murmured as she grabbed my dick through my jeans.

She started unbuckling my pants and I stopped her. *Why the fuck would I stop her*, I thought.

I ran my hand through her straight hair. "Zoey I want to make love to you, not fuck you, and not here. Because the things I want to do to you takes time." I glanced into Zoey's eyes caressing her face with the back of my hand. "I want you to wake up in my arms. You deserve more than this."

I stood her on her feet. She looked at me confused. "Baby, don't worry, it will be worth the wait. Now, how did you get here?"

"Stacey drove us."

"I'm going to have my friend Eric drive them home. Don't worry about him, he'll make sure Jeff follows him so he can get home."

"And you Zoey are coming with me. But wait, shit, only if you want to?"

"Yes Brandon, I want to," she smirked.

I opened the bedroom door only to hear the loud music and voices bouncing off the walls throughout the house. I pulled her by the hand down the hall past onlookers. Zoey walked behind me hugging me from behind. She ran her hands up the front of my shirt feeling my abs. I normally never let this happen, but Zoey can do as she pleases. The women gawked at her with disapproval as we walked through the house. She came back around to my side as we walked down the stairs.

"What was that about?" I asked with a smile.

"I just wanted to mess with them. Earlier I overheard a couple of the girls talking. They said you are not the relationship type and you were a dog. They went on to say you would probably just fuck me later and they would never see me again. So since they would never see me again I decided to have a little fun just to fuck with them."

When we got to the bottom of the stairs, I stood in front of her looking a little upset. Nevertheless, it's my fault because I asked her here. I should have just asked her out on a date instead.

"Zoey, knowing what they said you still want to go home with me?" I asked perplexed.

"Yes. Who said that's not all I want, too."

"Is that all you want?" I asked looking vulnerable.

She looked up in to my eyes. "How about we work on getting to know each other. I don't think we should discuss this here," she stated looking around the room.

"Alright, let's talk to your friends and get out of here," I said.

I was so pissed I'm sure my face was beet red. They had some nerve to look at her like that or say shit about her. They had no fucking idea what my intentions towards her were. They were mad because I chose her over them and truthfully, they didn't understand why.

CHAPTER SEVEN

BRANDON

We walked out to my truck in silence. I opened the passenger door of my Range Rover for her. I sat behind the steering wheel for a moment, then looked over at her.

"What's wrong?" Zoey asked.

I turned to her. "Listen, I do have sex with a lot of different women. Many of them were in the Frat house. Look, I like you a lot. I don't know why I like you over all the other women, but it's you. At this moment, I'm not interested in another woman. If we both decide after a couple of dates that we don't want to see each other, fine. Then that's it."

"Wait, hold on, who said we will make it past tonight," she said.

"Baby, trust me, we will," I assured her as we drove away.

"Let's change the subject. Are you rich," Zoey asked blatantly.

"Yes. Why?"

"Just wondered how you're able to drive an expensive truck like this, also because you attend Harvard. I recall you mentioned your tuition is paid and you are almost finished with medical school. Which means you're not making a doctor's salary yet."

"Does it make a difference?" I asked.

"No just wondered. I just remember when I shook your hand the other day it was smooth like you never performed manual labor," she said looking over at me.

"Well, I come from a long list of doctors, and even though I could be anything I wanted, I still chose to be a doctor. My grandfather expects my kids and my kid's kids to carry on the tradition."

"Do you have kids?" asked Zoey.

"No. Do you?"

"No," she responded looking out the window.

I wanted to ask her if her future plans included getting married and having kids, but she changed the subject again.

"My favorite season is spring. What's yours?"

"I love summer! Just enjoying the sun against my skin is good enough for me. I also love water sports, camping, and hunting. I know you like ice skating, but do you like camping?"

"I don't know, I've never been. I am open to the experience."

"Well stick with me baby, I'll have you all over this world," I winked.

We pulled into the parking garage of my condo. I opened her door, took her hand in mine, and proceeded to my condo on the top floor. She didn't make eye contact with me in the elevator. After exiting the elevator, I pulled her close to me as we continued down to the end of the hall, kissing the top of her head. When we got to my door, I put my key in the lock and I pulled her in front of me. I looked down at her and I immediately indulged her beautiful purple lips as I turned the key opening my door. She stepped in and looked around my spacious home.

"It's beautiful!" she said with a smile.

"What would you like to drink?" I asked.

"Something strong," said Zoey.

"Two scotches on the rocks coming right up."

She walked around looking at my family photos and my artwork. I walked over and grabbed her hand pulling her to the kitchen.

"Have a seat," I said.

I got on my knees in front of her, removed her shoes, and then rubbed her feet a bit. She watched me while drinking her scotch. I couldn't help but to laugh as she tried to tolerate the burn of the alcohol going down her throat.

"You said you wanted something strong to drink," I said as I stood up to kiss her lips.

"Are you trying to forget about our night?" I quizzed.

"No! It's just been a long time since I've had sex."

"I promise to take it slow." I assured her.

I pulled her to her feet.

"I bet I know what will make you happy!" I said as I pulled her up in my arms carrying her to my bedroom.

"Wait, my drink," she said.

"Don't worry about it. I'll bring it in soon," I replied setting her on the bed. I ran to retrieve our drinks and her shoes. I closed my bedroom door, passed her the drink, and placed her shoes in my closet. I sat next to her while we drank our scotch.

"Zoey I want more from you than just sex," I replied while kissing her ear and rubbing her back.

"I only want sex," she whispered.

"I'm not buying it."

I licked her from the base of her neck up to her chin. I stood in front of Zoey, then stripped down completely naked. I helped her to remove her dress, bra, and panties. Zoey's eyes widened when she observed my manhood then her eyes met mine.

"Don't worry baby I won't hurt you. I need you to put your stilettos back on for this."

I retrieved her stilettos, bent down, and put them back on her feet.

I pulled Zoey up off the bed and leaned down capturing her lips within mine. I sucked on her bottom lip, down the side of her neck, and back to her lips. The harder I pressed my lips into hers the further my dick rose to the occasion. It pressed against her stomach while our moaning turned to groaning. I released her lips only to take her by the hand over to the mirror in the corner of my room. I pulled her in front of me so our reflections stared back at us.

"When was the last time a man pleased you?"

"Years," she whispered.

"Hmm," I stated. "That's all about to change. I want to be the man to please you, if you'll let me," I said to her looking into her eyes.

I didn't give her a chance to respond, I took her lips within mine while placing both my hands on her breasts, massaging firmly.

I smirked, "I'm going to make you cum now. Do not close your eyes or take your eyes off of yourself. Do you understand?" I commanded while looking at her in the mirror.

"Yes," she affirmed.

I slid my hands down both sides of her beautiful brown body.

This woman oozes sex.

"Zoey, I can't wait to learn all of your cum faces." I affirmed as I looked deep into her eyes.

I moved my hand from her thigh to her mound. I traced my finger through the barely there hair, slipped my index finger down into her pussy hole then slid my finger through her wet trenches with ease.

"Baby did you cum without me?" I asked biting down on her ear slightly.

"No," she breathed.

"Zoey you do something to me that I can't explain."

"Same here," she said smiling.

I put my thumb in her mouth while I played with her clit. I watched her suck my thumb while I drove her crazy with my other hand.

"Zoey baby, are you ready to cum?"

I removed my thumb from her mouth so she could answer.

"Yes." Her eyes squinted, she clenched her teeth together as she rode her first orgasm. I placed my two soaking wet fingers into my mouth, licking them clean while she watched with lustful eyes.

I looked into her eyes through the mirror. "Zoey you taste so sweet. I will be tongue fucking that beautiful pussy of yours," I stated while I wrapped her in my arms. There is something special about you, Zoey Robinson."

"You said you weren't going to fuck me."

"Sweetheart, that's just one component of it. Tonight is about us getting to know each other sexually. Tomorrow I'll get into your brain, tonight your body."

"Brandon," she said looking at me with pain behind her eyes.

I don't know who hurt her but I have to make it right. No woman walking this earth should have to go through that, especially this one. I'm trying desperately not to fall hard for her, but I can't help it. I just know this is the woman I want, nobody else. I only want to please her.

"Brandon what's wrong?" she asked turning to face me. She ran her hand down the side of my face so tenderly.

I had to have her now. I grabbed her face and sent my lips crashing into hers repeatedly.

"I need you Zoey."

Shit this woman is making me weak.

"Baby, I'm here," she replied.

"Zoey, I need you to leave whatever you've done with other men out of this room, and I will leave what I've done with other women out as well." I picked her up into my arms and carried her over to my bed. "It's just about me and you."

She smiled at me as if she was relieved. I wasn't expecting that. I laid her down and hovered over her, looking into those big brown eyes.

"Stand up," she commanded.

I stood at the foot of the bed. Zoey came up on her knees in front of me. She put her finger in her mouth, looking over my body to see where she wanted to start. She ran her hand over my chest and abs, then kissed my chin down to my nipples. She rested her hands on my hips while she twirled her tongue around each of my nipples continuously. She jumped out of the bed and drank some of her now watered down scotch, returning to stand behind me. I felt her hands on my arms and something cold go down the middle of my back. The sensation was nice. The cold sensation went all the way down to the small of my back. She set her empty glass down then walked up onto my bed standing in front of me.

"Take me," she demanded.

Shit, I obliged. I swooped her up into my arms laying her back down on the bed, pulling her underneath me to the top of the bed. My masculine room swallowed us whole, all the perfect furniture meant nothing unless it was going to serve a purpose. I reached over into my nightstand drawer pulling out a magnum condom. She watched as I sat back on my knees rolling it down my shaft. Zoey in turn sat up grabbed my dick stroking it up and down, leaned forward and kissed the head of my dick then looked into my eyes.

"Uh uh, not now. Not saying I don't want you to do that, but not right now," I said as I pushed her back down on the bed. "I need to taste every inch of your body."

I kissed her lips, sucked on her neck, continued down to her beautiful 36c size breasts. Pretty sure, that's the size, since I've seen so many in my day. I ran my tongue all over her breasts. I sucked on each nipple until they were hard and at attention. Zoey placed her hands in my curly brown and blonde mane. I kissed the sides of her stomach down to her belly button. She giggled when I licked her belly button' letting me know it was a sensitive spot for her. I slowly kissed and licked her thighs down to her feet. I wanted to please her in every way. I sat up on my knees again, pushing her legs open so I can see her pretty pussy. Her brown exterior had been hiding her pink center. I dove right in. I licked from her ass to her clit and back again. I used my fingers to pull back her folds so I could suck on her pussy.

"Brandon," she screamed.

"Scream as loud as you want to baby."

I felt like I was home. I couldn't get enough of the way she tasted. I watched in amazement as her wetness pooled to the surface and I lapped it up. I caught her third orgasm between my teeth as I clinched her clit. It was like a waterfall. I have never seen that happen before. It was almost as if she couldn't turn it off. I love the effect I have on her as I watched her body convulse then I drank all of her again. I need to watch her cum one more time as I please her with my mouth. I know I mentioned before that I don't eat much pussy. It's not that I didn't like to, I guess I had been waiting for the right one; and I found her.

"Damn baby, your pussy taste so good," I moaned.

I placed my lips against her pussy then I sucked each inch. It was happening again as if a volcano was about erupt. I licked and sucked, then sucked her clit. She lost total control. I gripped her legs tighter with my arms. I wanted her to be free with me.

"Brandon come here," she breathed.

I didn't get my chance to tongue fuck her. I will get another chance later. I wiped my mouth slowly with the back of my hand before leaning down and kissing her lips. I pushed my tongue into her mouth just as I slid my dick inside her.

"Oh," she moaned against my lips as she tried getting adjusted to my size, but once she did, that was it. She squeezed my ass, I then placed her hands up over her head with one hand and grabbed her leg with the other. *I don't want to come quick but this woman has pussy whipped me. She is so fucking tight*, I thought. I moved in a circular motion, pleasing us both.

"Brandon right there," she murmured then bit down on her bottom lip. I released her hands. She wrapped her shaky arms around my neck.

"Zoey are you ok?"

"Um hum," she responded as she threw her head back. I continued taking long strokes back and forth. I gripped her ass cheek with one hand and took it home. I waited for her to say she's cumming as I pushed harder and faster inside her.

"Zoey, cum for me baby!" And just like that, she did. We were dripping wet with sweat. I looked down at her as I caressed her face with one hand and my other hand gripping her ass tighter as I thrust back and forth inside her until I came.

"Um," I grunted out.

"Shit Zoey, I think that may have been just about the best pussy I have ever had," I said falling to her side trying desperately to catch my breath. I pulled her into my arms kissing her beautiful full lips.

"I think we may have met our match. Because baby that was amazing!" said Zoey.

Zoey reached in the drawer for another condom. She took the old one off throwing it to the floor. She rolled the new condom down my dick, sat on my stomach while she stroked my staff up and down, then eased down on it slowly before finding her rhythm.

I watched her ride me like a bull. Damn, this woman knows just how to please me. She moved her ass in a circle then bounced up and down on my dick as she ran her hands through her hair then over her breasts. I grabbed her ass trying so hard not to cum.

"Brandon, cum for me," she whispered.

And just like that I did. She eased off my dick and into my arms.

"Brandon, I don't have sex anymore for a reason," she whispered.

"We will discuss that later. I do have one question for you. Do you like me a little or a lot?" I asked smiling at her.

She looked into my grey eyes. "Too damn much!"

"Well Zoey, I believe you have made my month. Just know the feeling is mutual," I said running my hand through her hair and holding her tight as we fell to sleep.

∞

The next morning, I woke up in a panic when I didn't see Zoey lying next to me. I smelled bacon in the air. I can't help but to smile at the thought of her cooking for me. I threw on a pair of boxers and I walked into the living room where I watched Zoey from afar. She's wearing my Harvard t-shirt and listening to music through her ear buds. Not sure how though. I started to approach her but then she started singing and it was just too funny. She waved the spatula in the air while she danced. I didn't want to startle her.

"Zoey!" I shouted

She didn't respond, just kept dancing. I walked up behind her pulling her close so she could feel my morning hard on.

I removed one of her earbuds and kissed the side of head. "Good morning baby."

She smiled up at me. I pulled up the shirt. She had her cell phone clipped to the inside of her panties. I ran my hand down the inside front of her panties to greedily feed on her wetness. I pushed the two hot skillets to the stove's cold back burners.

"Hey I was in the middle of cooking our breakfast!" she stated.

"I know baby," I breathed.

"Do you want me to stop?" I questioned.

She shook her head no against my chest. I gently circled my middle finger over her clit. Zoey started to moan.

"Brandon, I'm cumming!"

"Spread your legs baby," I whispered in her ear.

She obeyed. I continued on my mission to make her cum. I ran my finger back and forth in her folds causing her to moan louder.

"Don't hold back baby!"

Zoey came hard. I could feel her breathing heavily against my chest. I turned her around to face me, picked her up, lying her on the counter top. I behaved like a cave man, taking what I felt is now mine. I have no intentions of sharing her. I snatched off her earbuds and panties at once placing them on the counter, I got down on my knees and licked her center making sure I don't leave one drop of her juices behind. Finally, it's time to tongue fuck this chocolate beauty. I pushed my tongue inside her greedily, tongue fucking the daylights out of her. Her small frame rocked back and forth against the granite counter top.

"Brandon, Brandon, ummm it feels so fuckkking good!" she yelled as she came in my mouth.

I stood to my feet and wiped my mouth as I stared at her.

"Your pussy taste so fucking good!"

Zoey looked down at my huge boner. She climbed down off the counter, pulled my boxers down, grabbed my dick, and began to stroke back and forth before taking me into her mouth. Shit, it felt amazing! Her lips moved gracefully back and forth. She slowed her pace to move her tongue in a circular motion around the head of my dick. My right hand rested on the countertop and my other in her hair.

"Fuck Zoey, Shit! That feels so good!" I moaned.

I had to sound like a bitch, but there was no way to explain how she could make me feel this way. I can't let her know that I would give her anything the way she's pleasing me right now. I tried to pull back but she gripped my ass tighter. She moaned as she sucked sending me over the top. I came hard, the hardest I ever have while getting my dick sucked. She sat back on her knees, swallowed, got up off the floor, and continued cooking. She didn't say a word. She just drank down her orange juice.

"What's wrong?" she asked.

"Nothing. You know what, I'm lying. You sucked my dick like it's a job, and you go back to cooking."

"I felt I needed to please you."

I wasn't happy with her answer. I sat down in a chair on the other side of the counter. *Let me think about what I'm going to say before I start yelling, I thought.*

I walked back over to her. "Zoey don't ever do that to me again if you don't like to do it. I want you to like it. Baby, who made you do that?"

"I would rather not say," she said sadly.

I felt like throwing the skillets across the room.

I grabbed her by her arms to look at me. "I want you to know that yes, that was the best blow job I have ever had, but don't do it again unless you want to. I won't ever, I repeat ever, make you do something you don't want to do. Alright?"

"Ok," she smiled. She pulled me down toward her, gently kissing my lips.

"I did like it, I just thought it was the right thing to do."

"Zoey I don't know why this is happening, or how, but I'm falling for you fast."

"Me too, Brandon."

"Oh, I forgot to tell you my friends said thanks for making sure they got home safe," said Zoey.

"That's good to hear," I smiled.

After breakfast and a shower together, I took Zoey back to her place to change and pick up some clothes. She agreed to spend the rest of the weekend with me. We stepped into her small but cute, girly apartment. I shuffled around looking for family photos, but there weren't any, just photos of the ocean and one of her holding a black Labrador dog.

I could hear Zoey moving around in her bedroom.

"Is this your dog?" I asked loudly.

"No," she shouted.

"It's my grandmother's."

I sat down on the couch and retrieved my cell phone from my pocket. I looked up my notes for Monday's test.

About 30 minutes later, she stood before me.

"I have my overnight bag and I'm ready to go."

"Let me take your bag. You look beautiful!"

Zoey had on tight fitted blue jeans, a red blouse, a pair of flats and her hair pulled up into a long ponytail. I tell you, I wanted her right then and there. I told my dick down boy. We'll get that later.

"Why do you say it like you just saw me for the first time?" she asked.

"Every time you wear your hair different, it is the first time for me," I said smiling and giving her a peck on the lips as we stepped onto the elevator.

CHAPTER EIGHT

ZOEY

I can't believe this guy asked me to spend the entire weekend with him. Shit, I can't believe I accepted. Shit, why not? This man satisfied me like no other. Wait, I'm getting ahead of myself.

Brandon interrupted my thoughts. "Zoey is there any station in particular you want to listen to on the radio?"

"No Brandon. Play a station you normally listen to."

"Alright."

Heavy metal blasted loudly through the speakers. I cut him a look as if to say, are you fucking kidding?

He turned the music down. "I'm just messing with you! I will play some new country."

That sounds a lot better. Brandon was beating his hand against the steering wheel and singing along while he drove. I can't help but look at him and smile. He looked back at me and winked. God, I'm telling you I could fuck him right now. I look forward to the time we will spend together. This morning we decided to go ice-skating. Where was I? Yeah, so I decided to show up at the Frat party. I mean, what did I have to lose. I hadn't had sex in a long time. I admit I initially was going to attempt to hold out until he kissed my lips later that night. I thought, what the hell! I have to see what he has to offer below the belt. It could only be good or bad, so I just decided to take a chance. I mean, hell, I I took a chance on the last two lame asses.

When I first arrived, my friends said they wanted to dance. I offered to get us drinks. I couldn't believe my eyes when I walked up to the bar. He was making eyes with another woman. Now why was I jealous? The woman spoke to me when Brandon's eyes fell on me. She said I must be real special to make Brandon nervous.

Clearly she was fucking him. The way they stared at each other said it all.

I had to get my mind right and look at it for what it was, a hook up. When he found me on the dance floor a little while later I admit my heart skipped a beat. After all, this man is drop dead gorgeous. His beautiful curly brown hair, grey eyes, and his handsome chiseled features are enough to make any woman drop her panties. What I wasn't expecting was the kiss. He kissed me as if he had missed me. Like he hadn't seen me in months, and it had only been a few days. He told me he would catch up with me soon. He had to help a friend. While I walked around the party, looking for my friends it appeared most of the women were whispering to each other and shooting me dirty looks. When I walked into the kitchen, I overheard a woman say to her friend, "Brandon isn't the settling down type he'll fuck and get rid of her like he does all the others."

He has a reputation of being the Bed King, I thought.

Oh, so they think I'm like them? Hard up pining away for the great doctor Asher II? Well I'll have you to know I'm not. I never told Brandon all the things they said about me. Really what did it matter? It was a one-night stand. I didn't give a fuck what they were saying. *As far as I was concerned they could have him back the next day!* But that wasn't the case, I thought. I sit here next to him today on our second date. Brandon wants to spend more time with me. I won't look a gift horse in the mouth, I like hanging out with him, among other things.

Back to the night of the Frat party. We left the party and went back to his condo. That night Brandon showed me how attentive he could be to me. He wanted to please me, make love to me. Maybe that was his thing to make women feel special, then let them go. I don't know, but I didn't get that vibe from him. I felt like he was being sincere. So now, I felt like the asshole for not being able to see him after this weekend. Shit, this man wants a wife and kids and I can't give him either. I am a loner. I don't deserve happiness after what I did to my mother. My psychiatrist says I do. She told me that I was the one who was molested, robbed of my innocence, and forced into womanhood before my time. I guess I have a long way to go in therapy. I wish I could have a man like Dr. Asher. Let me just tell you, this man is going to make some woman the happiest woman in the world.

He brought me to orgasm after orgasm last night. It was amazing. He couldn't get enough of eating my pussy. Shit that man licked my pussy like no man has ever done. He moaned and groaned, not being able to get enough of me. It makes me wet just thinking about last night. I wasn't expecting his dick to be so big. I had never seen one that thick and long. He made me feel relaxed, allowing me to adjust to his size. I started biting my nails just thinking how he told me he couldn't get enough of me. I think when I rode his dick that's what did it for him. He started confessing all kinds of things to me. God, this man is fine!

This morning I woke before him. I watched him sleep for a good fifteen minutes. He looked so peaceful. He never let me go that night. I can't believe he held me tight all night long. I grabbed his Harvard t-shirt out of his closet and slipped it on. I was drowning in it but I didn't have anything else to put on. I'm 5'5, he's 6'3. I walked into his kitchen to see if he had any breakfast food. Before I made breakfast, I made myself a cup of tea and sat in a huge chair in front of his large picture window. The view from his condo is beautiful. He has a similar view from his bedroom. I sat in the chair and cried into my tea. Mad at the world, pissed that my mother's men came on to me, then her husband molested me. Why did I have to get a raw deal? Did I really think that I deserved happiness? Hell no!

Can you see me telling him 'Brandon I want to tell you about my life, tell you how I was ruined and had no chance of being with a good man'. I would tell him how I was molested and then that would be it, he would look at me with pity and re-think wanting to marry me. This is why I will never tell him. I don't want to see the disappointment splattered across his face. Second option, he still wants to be with me and wants to have kids. I can't do that. I can't bring a child into this world. I won't bring a child into this world to get molested. I just won't! Therefore, this is why I won't get to marry a man like Brandon Christopher Asher II.

Let me continue. He came into the kitchen kissing my neck. Making me feel wanted and adored. He took me right there in the kitchen. He tongue fucked me to ecstasy. It was again amazing. I couldn't believe when I repaid the favor, he got mad because I was just trying to do the honorable thing. When he told me I didn't have to do anything I didn't want to, I fell in love with him. Nevertheless, I would never tell him.

"Zoey, we're here."

 "Great," I said wiping my face free of tears. I tried not to look at him, but he grabbed my chin and looked into my eyes.

"Zoey, you're with me now, whatever happened with those assholes before us is over baby. I only want you."

I caressed his face and had no words.

I broke our silence. "Hey let's get in there and see if I still got it on the ice Come on!"

Brandon got our skates while I went to the bathroom to freshen up. I made myself have fun. Which really wasn't hard with him. I was trying to fight the feeling of sadness that kept reminding me that I had to tell him I couldn't ever see him again.

"Brandon I might fall but I am going to see if I can still do it."

"Do what?" he inquired.

"You'll see," I exclaimed.

I skated out to the middle of the floor and attempted to do a figure 8. He smiled at me from ear to ear. I skated around to get familiar with my skates and then I twirled around in the middle of the floor and did a perfect figure 8. All the onlookers and Brandon clapped for me. I noticed the twinkle in his eye. He really does adore me. Shit, what am I to do? I skated right into his arms giving him the biggest kiss. We played around for another hour. I had the best time.

We arrived at Wicked Fire Kissed pizza in Denham. We were seated at large booth. The waitress gave us menus and extra time to order.

"Brandon I'm ready to order."

"What size pizza?"

"Hear me out! Let's order an extra-large pizza." I said smiling at him.

He laughed and winked at me. "I'll give you extra-large something else later!"

"I'm counting on it!" I winked back.

"Seriously I would like pepperoni, ham, onions, black olives, mushrooms, and anchovies!"

Brandon scrunched his face up at me.

"What, you don't like those toppings?" I asked.

"Zoey, that's disgusting!"

"I'm just joking. I actually want pepperoni, extra cheese, and mushrooms."

"That's better, let's order a large half and half. I want all meat on my half."

"Brandon that sounds good, too," I smiled.

"Baby we can share," he said leaning over the table to kiss my nose.

"Ok," I replied as my heart skipped a beat again. Another public display of affection.

Brandon placed our order.

"So tell me everything there is to know about you."

"Brandon there is not much to tell."

"Let's start with our favorite colors, favorite sports played in high school, favorite TV show, snacks, food, and sweets."

"Alright, I loved being a cheerleader, but I also loved soccer. My favorite color is red, TV shows Greys Anatomy, Vampire Diaries, House Hunters, and Real Housewives. My favorite food fried shrimp, snacks caramel popcorn, and Godiva chocolate. Your turn!"

"My favorite sport was Lacrosse, favorite colors navy blue and grey."

"Ah huh, I see why your favorite color is grey. That shirt brings out your grey eyes," I laughed.

"Real funny Zoey, you are such a corn ball!"

"Come sit next to me."

"Brandon, no," I said as my eyes widened.

"You either come over here now or I will embarrass you."

"Fine!"

I sat down next to him and he pulled me close to him. He gazed into my eyes and captured my lips with in his. *Fuck I can't wait for him to be inside me again,* I thought.

"Are you two ready to order?" asked the waitress.

I didn't even notice she had walked over to our table. Brandon placed our order.

"So where was I?" he asked interlocking our fingers together. He continued to tell me what he loves.

"I love the Walking Dead, of course watching all things sports, too. I have season tickets to the New England Patriots, Boston Bruins hockey, Boston Red Sox, and the Boston Celtics.

"Wow, you don't love sports do you?" I joked.

"You better get used to it because I will be taking you with me," he said smiling.

"Anyway, my favorite snack potato chips, Snickers bars, shit I love junk food! To think I wanted to be a doctor."

We laughed.

"My favorite foods of all are pizza and Italian."

"Aww, great our food is here. Thanks Theresa!"

"No problem B Dawg." She smiled as she walked away.

"She just flirted with you right in front of me," I said as my mouth opened wide and my eyes widened.

"What's the matter, are you jealous?"

I just smiled.

He leaned his head close to my ear. "I only have eyes for you and that beautiful brown pussy of yours."

I swear I came a little bit just from the sound of his voice whispering in my ear. At this moment, I want to take him into the bathroom and fuck his brains out. I am so hot right now.

He looked into my eyes. "I admit I have been a dick for a long time. But you make me want more out of life than just my career."

"Brandon, I can't give you what you want."

"Alright, then I'll take you home after we eat," he said sadly.

"Brandon I don't want to go home. I enjoy being with you," I admitted taking his hands into mine.

"Zoey, then why are you pushing me a way?"

"I don't deserve happiness. I've done some things in my life that won't allow me to be happy."

"Zoey, so tell me how you really feel about me?"

"Damn it Brandon! I will hurt you!"

"So let's stop seeing each other right now," he beseeched.

I realized it's a little harder than I thought. I decided to keep seeing him from time to time. I mean shit, give up that mind blowing sex? I don't think so. I will have to keep him hanging on a bit. I reached under his shirt and felt his abs, kissed his chin up to his lips and then he kissed me back. I got him, he's smiling at me again.

"Zoey what are you doing to me?"

I just smiled as I gazed into his eyes. It feels like we are in our own bubble. No one else exists, until someone approached the table.

"Hey B Dawg, what's up man?"

Brandon stood and shook the man's hand. "Ryan, what's up dude? Let me introduce you to Zoey Robinson."

"Nice to meet you Ryan."

"Zoey nice to meet you."

"Have a seat," said Brandon.

"Where's Melissa?"

"She's coming she had to run to the restroom."

"Would you like some pizza?" I asked.

"No thanks. Just going to grab a beer then we will go over to our table when it's ready."

I am now uncomfortably nervous. I feel selfish because I just want Brandon all to myself.

Ryan flagged down the waitress. "Hey Ryan!"

"Hey Theresa, let me order two Bud Lights."

"Coming right up!"

I took a bite of pizza hoping to stay out of the hot seat.

"So Zoey, are you from Massachusetts?"

No chance of staying out the hot seat. I chew fast then pick up a napkin to wipe my mouth. "No, I am from Charleston, South Carolina."

"Oh, a Southern girl," he stated looking at Brandon.

"Hello everyone," a woman said taking a seat next to Ryan.

"My name is Melissa," she said reaching out to shake my hand.

I instantly feel boxed in and like I'm under a spotlight.

"Zoey, nice to meet you!" I said shaking her hand.

I smiled.

"Nice to meet you, too."

Theresa dropped off beers for Ryan, Melissa and another one for Brandon.

"Melissa, I just found out Zoey is from Charleston, South Carolina."

"I love Charleston! What made you come here, the weather is much better there?" said Melissa.

I lied. "School."

"Oh, what school?" she asked.

"Boston University."

I feel my hands starting to sweat.

CHAPTER NINE

ZOEY

"How do your parents feel about you being so far away?" asked Melissa.

I froze. I don't know how to respond. What do I say, I don't have parents? Do I let them know my Mom and I don't talk anymore?

"Um, you know what, I need to run to the restroom I'll be back," I replied to her, never looking at Brandon.

I really want to run right out the door and not look back. I stepped into the empty restroom and swiftly moved to the sink. I turned on the cold water and splashed water on my face.

I looked at my reflection in the mirror. I see the argument I had with my mother clear as day.

"Get the fuck out of my house! You are dead to me!" My mother yelled pointing her finger in my face.

Let me go back a bit and tell you what happened the night of the Christmas Party. My grandmother caught me making that naughty face at Martin. She didn't say anything that night. I went over my grandmother's house that Friday for the weekend.

That Saturday morning I cooked breakfast for my grandfather and me. I placed a plate in front of her, one in front of me and took my seat.

"Zoey did you enjoy yourself at the Christmas party."

"Yes grandma it was cool!"

"What's going on between you and Martin?"

I started choking on my sausage link.

"Grandma I don't know what you are talking about," I chuckled.

She placed her hands over mine.

"Zoey why did you make that face at Martin?"

I immediately looked down at my plate. I didn't say a word I just forked through my eggs.

"Zoey I want answers now!" she demanded slamming her fist down on the table.

"I want to know what this face was about!" she said sternly, mimicking the face, I made at the Christmas party to Martin.

I was appalled with myself. My eyes were large as saucers.

"Now tell me what is going on child."

"Grandma, I can't!" I cried.

"Baby look at me," she said pulling my eyes up to meet hers.

"Grandma would never judge you. Remember when your mother's boyfriend tried to have sex with you?"

"Yes," I replied in a whisper. I looked away from her and just cried.

"Zoey! Is Martin trying to have sex with you?"

I didn't answer I just continued to cry.

"Zoey did he-touch you?"

I jumped up ran around the table sat on the floor and laid my head in my Grandmother's lap.

"Shush," she whispered running her hands through my hair.

"Baby it's going to be alright."

"Grandma he's been having sex with me for a year," I stated.

"Grandma gone take care of his ass!"

"Grandma you can't!"

"The hell you preach!"

"But Grandma he said he'll take everything away from my mother!"

"Baby don't you worry about nothing!" she affirmed pulling my chin up to look into her eyes.

I stand here today looking at myself in the mirror and smile at the thought of my Grandmother believing in me. It's important that I see my Psychiatrist this week. I haven't had to see her in a very long time. I don't feel like I'm up to being with Brandon today. I take a deep breath stroll out of the restroom. I can hear them laughing as I approach the table.

"It was very nice to meet you both. Something came up," I replied directing my answers to everyone at the table.

Brandon stood up in front of me, cupped my face making me look up into his beautiful grey eyes. He didn't say a word in that moment. He let go of my face to reach into his pocket.

"Here are the keys to my truck," he said opening my hand, placing the keys against my palm, closing it shut.

He placed his hands back on my face, "Please just give me a minute?"

"Alright," I replied. I didn't bother to look at his friends because I was so embarrassed.

I climbed into the passenger side of his truck and waited.

Five minutes later I watched Brandon walk across the parking lot towards me. He jumped into the truck and closed the door behind him. I already had the engine running.

He looked at me then looked straight ahead. "Why were you crying?"

"Because I don't have parents."

Brandon turned to me with a shocked expression across his face.

"Why didn't you tell me? Shit, I feel silly. I should have waited to introduce you to my friends.

I'm sorry," he said looking down.

I placed my finger under his chin lifting his head so his eyes could meet mines. "How could you know. I never planned to tell you. I'm flattered that you wanted your friends to meet me. I feel very special right now. Something I hadn't felt before; not from a man."

Brandon's eyes grew in size, "Baby, who hurt you?" he asked caressing my face.

I sighed. "Brandon this is why I'm no good for you I'm brok-." Brandon's lips slammed into mine. I didn't want him to release my lips.

Brandon stared tenderly into my eyes. "The hell you are. You are not broken. You are the most interesting woman I have ever met. I love being with you. Maybe because I have to work harder at impressing you, something I never had to do for any woman. They always take whatever I give. Zoey, I'm willing to wait for you to tell me your darkest secrets."

I sat back firm in my seat, folded my arms, and scrunched up my face. "God Brandon, don't you get it? There is no happy ending for me!"

"Why?" he asked.

"I will only tell you a little bit about me. I lost my father when I was five years old," I said as I started to cry. "It was just my mother and I for a long time," I stated, looking out the window.

"Let's just say I went through a tumultuous time when I was a teenager causing my mother to disown me. My grandmother took me in and I still have a relationship with my father's parents. What I went through as a teen was so traumatic that I still see a psychiatrist. However, it doesn't mean I'm crazy."

"Zoey I know you're not crazy."

"How do you know? Because you slept with me one night, held me all night long and I didn't go crazy on you. Is that what makes me not crazy in your eyes? Brandon, even though I'm not crazy I am really fucked up," I said looking over at him.

"Zoey."

"I'm sorry Brandon. Look, I don't have anything else planned. I just needed to get out of there."

"Great then I still have you to myself," he smiled.

Next thing I knew we were pulling into the parking lot of the Red Sox stadium. I didn't know if he had this planned or what, but I knew I was impressed. When he parked the truck, I jumped into his lap just to show him how happy he made me.

Is this what it's like to date someone? If it is, deep down I don't ever want it to stop, I thought.

I placed my lips over his deepening our kiss never wanting to let his lips go. I knew then my feelings were deepening for Brandon and that scared me.

"Thank you," I said.

"You are welcome, sweetheart," he smiled back.

When we exited the truck, he grabbed my hand and we walked inside the stadium. He looked over at me raising my hand up to meet his lips.

We approached the gate. "Thank you for joining us today Mr. Asher."

"Hello Mike. I would like you to meet my friend Zoey."

"Nice to meet you Zoey. This is pretty special, I've been working at the stadium since Brandon was a boy and through the years he's never brought a woman with him. You must be very special."

I blushed from ear to ear. "Thank you Mike, for the compliment, it is nice to meet you."

Brandon immediately took me over to a vendor to get me dressed in Red Sox gear. He bought 2 baseball caps and a Red sox button down shirt for me. He placed a cap on my head and one on his. We then stood in a long line for our refreshments.

I saw a woman running toward us from the corner of my eye.

"Mr. Asher, sir, you don't have to stand in line. I will take your order and bring it to your Sky Box," said the woman.

"Sharon that won't be necessary we're going to sit behind the dugout today."

"Sir let me see your tickets. Ok, please tell me your orders and I'll have it sent to your seats."

Brandon looked down at me in a state of confusion.

"I will take a Cherry Pepsi, cracker jacks, cotton candy, and a hot dog."

The woman wrote down my order. Brandon followed suit and placed his order.

"Emmanuel come here please!" said Sharon.

"I need you to escort Mr. Asher and his guest to their seats, they are in row A seats 21 and 22."

"Yes ma'am."

"Right this way," said Emmanuel.

Walking down to our seats, I looked out at the beautiful green grass on the field. The bases and diamond were still perfect. The smell of popcorn and hot dogs in the air brought a smile to my face. Right as we were about to be seated one of the players called out to Brandon.

"Hey Brandon what's going on man?" asked the player.

Brandon greeted him back.

"Bring your guest down so she can hit balls with us."

"Yes, that would be great!" I said smiling from ear to ear.

We sat so close to the field it was perfect! You could hear the player's conversations. It was so cool watching them leave the dugout. It was amazing! I couldn't stop smiling.

"Zoey I'm sorry for the fuss. My family has a long standing with the Red Sox. My grandfather's father provided the players medical attention in the past. Some of the players now have my father as their personal physician. My family's pictures are throughout the stadium. I guess you can say my family is a big deal here, that's the reason for the special treatment. They have known me since I was a boy. I put on a hat, hoping to fly under the radar. I didn't want to ask you if you wanted to sit in the Skybox because I thought it would overwhelm you. I'm trying to ease you into my flamboyant life," he said smiling awkwardly.

"Brandon, thanks for your thoughtfulness. The only thing I actually have a problem with is family. Everything else is fair game!" I turned Brandon's hat to the back, grabbed each side of his face, giving him a gentle kiss.

The next thing I know we were on the Jumbo Tron, and everyone around us was clapping. I placed my lips over his repeatedly. I just know I am kissing the most handsome man here.

CHAPTER TEN

ZOEY

From the moment we entered his condo we couldn't keep our hands off of each other.

"Brandon I need to take a shower," I said as I gave him another quick kiss.

"Is your roommate coming back tonight?" I asked.

"No he is gone for the weekend."

I unbuttoned my Red Sox shirt and slid it down my arms throwing it to the floor. Brandon threw his baseball cap on the chair then pulled his t-shirt over his head. I didn't take my eyes off his while I stripped down leaving a trail of clothes as I walked backwards towards the bedroom. Brandon swooped me up into his arms. I wrapped my arms around his head running my hands through the back of his hair. My head rested against his while our lips touched. He held me steady with his arms firmly under my ass.

"Zoey, baby, I don't want to go back to my old ways. I only want to be with you."

I'm shocked at his display of emotions. I lay flush against his washboard abs.

I tried to wiggle myself down from his strong embrace.

"Do you want me to fuck other women? Do you want me to do what I do to you, to them?"

"Brandon that's not fair. Please put me down?"

Once my feet were planted firmly on the floor I swiftly made my way into the bathroom. I turned on the shower, then stood there wrapping my hair in a ball on the top of my head. I watched Brandon sit on the bed warring with his thoughts. I stepped into the shower standing close to the water with my eyes closed letting the water beat against my brown skin. I opened my eyes just as Brandon entered the shower. He was huffing and puffing with a look of rage upon his face. His hair hung down in his eyes. He didn't say a word he just stared at me as I washed my body.

"Zoey, so all you want from me is sex?"

I smiled as I attempted to lather his chest with soap. He grabbed one of my wrists. The soap flew out of my hand hitting the shower floor.

"Stop Zoey, answer me," he demanded, pushing my back against the wall now holding both my wrists.

I stood there staring at him in silence.

"Zoey, I don't want anyone else to be with you. It would absolutely drive me nuts to think that another man was inside of what's mine," he confessed with a snarl.

"Brandon, let me go," I demanded with fury in my eyes.

He let my wrists go.

"Brandon, I am not yours. I am nobody's! I will not ever have a boyfriend, husband, or kids for that matter! It would be selfish of me to tell you how I want you to make love to me every night, and that I would kill a bitch if she came close to you! I don't want another man to ever touch me because no man will ever touch me the way that you do! Don't ever ask me about what I want because I don't matter, that is how bad I messed up my life," I said as I dropped my head and began sobbing.

"Zoey, baby I won't let you push me away. I don't know who fucked you over like this, but I'm not giving up on you. I want you here with me, always," he said running his fingers up and down my arm. So you would want to hurt another woman," he said smiling as he kissed my lips.

"Brandon I want you now." I said as I jumped up into his arms kissing his earlobe. "I need to feel you inside me," I whispered.

I slid my tongue deep into his mouth as I moaned for him. I wrapped my arms around his neck tight. He ran his hand down my ass then ran his fingers up and down my slit making me wetter. I looked into his grey eyes seeing his need for me. I slammed my lips into his again at the same time he plunged his long thick dick inside me. My head jerked back from the initial shock of him invading me. I quickly adjusted pushing myself up and down on his dick. He grabbed my ass as he groaned loudly pushing himself deeper into me.

"Oh Brandon! Yes! - Um! You feel so good," I moaned.

He breathed heavily into my neck. "Oh, shit your pussy is so tight and so goo-oood! I'm cumming!"

I locked my legs tighter around his waist. I felt myself beginning to convulse. "I'm cumming!" I screamed as my nails tore into his back.

Brandon slammed into me two more time as he came inside me. I gently kissed his lips.

Brandon blinked twice as he tried to catch his breath. He placed me down on the shower floor. I stepped back under the water to continue washing up. Brandon sat down on the shower floor watching me as I washed up. I stretched my hand out for his. He stood to his feet and joined me.

"Are you worried that you could get me pregnant? Because you can't, I'm on the shot. Listen Dr. Asher, right now I have you all to myself and I get to feel you inside me whenever I want," I said grabbing his manhood stroking it up and down. I looked up into his eyes. "Tonight I want you to fuck me good. Because you are the first man I've had in two years."

I stood there waiting for his response while he stood under the second showerhead washing up.

"Alright, it appears you're still upset with me." I stepped out of the shower grabbed a towel to dry off with and walked to the kitchen to pour myself a glass of water. Brandon was sitting on the bed with a towel wrapped around his waist when I returned to the bedroom. I stood in front of him drinking my water. He grabbed my glass and started drinking some of the water before handing it back to me.

"Monday, I want you to take me to work. We'll get tested before I start my shift. When was your last test?" he asked.

"Six months ago. And you?"

"Last month." he replied.

"My results showed I'm clean."

"I'm clean, too!" I said.

Brandon removed the glass from my hand, set it on the dresser, and then tossed me on the bed. He ripped the towel from my body and moved right down between my legs. I screamed his name then bit down on my bottom lip.

"Oh baby, don't stop!" I moaned as I ran my fingers through his hair.

The feeling of him licking me from my ass to clit was intense.

"Whose is it?" He groaned.

I didn't respond until he circled his tongue around my clit bringing my orgasm quickly to the surface.

"Whose is it?"

He had me. I couldn't help myself, he licked and sucked my pussy so good. Shit, it really was his. I wanted nothing to do with any other man. I was branded by Brandon.

He grabbed my left breast with one hand as he kept a tight grip on my right hip. My body shuddered against his tongue.

"Brandon, it's yours, always!" As soon as I said that he drove it home. I let go of his hair and I gripped the sheets hard.

Brandon finally came up for air watching me ride out my orgasm. He captured my heart and there was nothing I could do about it. He looked down at me as he hovered over me kissing my lips. His smile widened.

I moved from under his powerful stare. I got on all fours and pointed my ass to the sky just right. Brandon kneeled behind me, then leaned down licking my juices.

"Fuck you taste so good."

He eased back up and before I knew what hit me, he slammed into me. Then he pulled out and slammed into me again. I screamed so loud from the pain. "What was that for?"

"You told me you want me to fuck you, so that is what I'm doing."

"Brandon."

"Ok baby, I'll be gentle."

He pushed into me slowly, then picked up speed as he held my hips firmly.

He circled his dick inside me causing me to cum instantly. Brandon laid me down on my back kissing my ear.

"This pussy is the best I have ever had. Come here."

Brandon moved to the middle of the bed, he sat flat on the bed.

"Come sit on my dick."

I eased down on his dick while facing him.

"That's it, I want to see your face when you tell me your pussy is mine and no one else's."

I sat there on his lap, straddling him. He held my ass in his hands, moving me in a circular motion slow, then fast. He caused me to lose touch with reality while my arms laid loosely around his neck.

"It feels soooo good Brandon," I murmured. "Oh, you're hitting my sweet spot."

He knew he had me.

"Whose is it Zoey?" he asked still circling his dick inside me driving me absolutely crazy.

Now I understand why those women gave me those nasty looks. They wanted him to keep them cumming like this. Shit, I don't even think he gave them half of what he's giving me, since he said I was the first woman he ever made love to. I know I don't want to let him go. Could I be happy? Could I have the white picket fence and a family? I quickly drop those thoughts from my mind.

I felt my muscles tighten around his dick as I was cumming for the fifth time tonight. I breathed heavily trying to keep the words from exiting my mouth. However, it was too late. "I'm falling in love with you."

It was as if he had been waiting for me to say it since we arrived here tonight. His eyes rolled back in his head as he spit out words I didn't expect.

"I love you Zoey," he groaned against my mouth as he exploded inside me.

We sat there a minute fixated on each other. I pulled myself off of his dick. He grabbed my body pulling me close as we laid down together. He looked into my eyes as he smoothed my sex hair down that had completely fallen out of the bun a long time ago. He placed his lips over mine, pulling them into his. He held me in his arms as we fell asleep.

∞

I woke a few hours later watching him sleep with his mouth partially opened and his brownish blonde hair tousled across his forehead. I'm in love with this man already, how can this be? Shit I don't know, but I love everything about him. I could lay here with him every night and wake to his handsome face every morning. I kissed his lips then slowly got out of the bed. I grabbed my bed t-shirt and shorts from my bag throwing them on. I used the bathroom then I slowly made my way to the kitchen to make myself a large cup of tea. I took a seat in my favorite spot of the spacious condo. The big red chair sat right in front of the window perfectly, so I could see the entire city. At night it is the most beautiful view you have ever seen. The skyline is perfect. I smiled as I sipped my tea before setting the cup down on the small table next to me. My happy thoughts were severely interrupted when I thought about how my mother reacted to what my step- father did to me. I couldn't help but cry when I vividly heard those words. "You're dead to me!" A whimper escaped my lips. I pulled my legs in tight, crying uncontrollably. I felt a gentle touch on my leg. He shushes me. I pulled my face from my knees to see Brandon in front of me on his knees. He was bare chested, wearing only pajama bottoms. I tell you I looked a hot mess, but you would never know by the way this man looked at me with such love and admiration in his eyes. He pulled several tissues from the box wiping away the tears and snot running down my face. I grabbed a couple of tissues from the box that was resting on the arm of the chair. I blew my nose, Brandon took the tissues from me and put them on the table.

"Stand up," he said softly.

He sat down in the chair and pulled me into his lap. He positioned me so I could still see the city.

"Baby tell me what's wrong."

I wanted to tell him everything, but I just couldn't, I only told him a little.

"I remembered when my mother told me I was dead to her. It hurts."

"Of course it does sweetheart," he whispered in my ear.

I sat there wrapped in his loving arms. God, I must be dreaming because how did I get a man like this?

"I'm here for you Zoey," he said as I fell asleep.

CHAPTER ELEVEN

BRANDON

Zoey has been the best distraction a man could have. I wouldn't let Zoey out of my sight for fear she wouldn't come back. Zoey and I have been together for two months now. I had her drop me off at work every day. I let her run her errands and go to work. If our schedules conflicted, I would take my family's car service home. Something else I hid from Zoey. I kept thinking she'd freak if she knew how rich I actually am. Tonight I'm going to have her drive me out to my parents so I can get another car for myself to drive. The car service is great and all, especially when I work late, but I like to drive around the city sometimes and clear my head.

My best friend Ryan moved out this week. He said me and Zoey were keeping him up with our loud sexcapades. The day after our first Red Sox game together, our night became very intense. It still hurts my heart thinking how this beautiful woman feels she doesn't deserve happiness. I am in love with Zoey. I said it before and I will say it again. Let me get the opportunity to put hands on the motherfucker who fucked up my Zoey's head. Her past has put a damper on our future. Deep down I believe Zoey is my girlfriend, but she won't let me call her that.

Let's go back to that night after the baseball game. My thought process was really fucked up! Zoey told me she didn't want another man. She only wanted me. Zoey went on to say she didn't want me to be with another woman but in the same breath she said she couldn't be serious with me. That woman jumped up into my arms and I blacked out. I didn't think of the possible dangers of having unprotected sex with her, and to be honest I didn't care, I needed to be inside of her. Zoey and I have this burning desire for each other when we are together. Shit I made love to her every chance I got for breakfast, lunch, dinner, and dessert. I couldn't get enough of her. Zoey is like a drug to me. I have to have her at all times. I believe I've accomplished my goal of learning all of her cum faces. I sometimes woke Zoey out of her sleep just so I could taste her sweet pussy. This has never happened to Brandon C. Asher II.

I started spoiling Zoey. I found the best hair stylist in the city to do her hair. I took her shopping for an entire wardrobe. New watches, a dainty little necklace to remind her of my love for her and a beautiful Pandora charm bracelet. The next piece of jewelry I buy for her will be a ten carat diamond engagement ring. My parents will be happy to meet the woman I've been spending thousands of dollars on. We got our tests back two weeks after having unprotected sex together. The test results read we were both free of any STD's. I was so happy to keep going raw inside of her. Shit her pussy really is the best I ever had. I don't think she believes me, which is good, we should probably keep it that way. Zoey pulled up in front of the hospital right on time.

"Hey baby," I said as I threw my bag into the back seat. I kissed her tantalizing lips and marveled over her perfect coily hair. Her hair is styled just the way I like it. Just looking at her beautiful brown face makes my dick hard. I typed my parents address into the GPS as I listened to her tell me about her day. *I have to find a way to break her walls down*, I thought.

I planned to ask for hand in marriage one day. I need her to be able to trust me enough to tell me her deepest darkest secrets and know that I won't leave her.

"Can you pull over right here for just a minute? Zoey I need to tell you something. Please don't be upset with me."

She threw the gearshift in park, folded her arms, and scrunched up her face. "I'm listening."

I turned to look at her. "Ok, I haven't been completely honest with you. Ok, here it goes. My family is part owners of the Red Sox, that is the real reason for all the commotion when we arrived at the stadium. The employees really have known me since I was a child. However, people know me as Mr. Red Sox because when I was eighteen they called me out to the field to hit the first ball of the night. I stepped up to the plate, the pitcher pitched the ball to me, and I hit it out of the park. They know me all over the city for that one play.

"Another thing, when I turn thirty, I am instantly a billionaire."

"A billionaire doctor?" she asked.

"Yes. I come from old money, as people sometimes say. So truthfully I never have to work. I choose to. My mother and father are laid back, not snooty. They try to be regular people, not let money run their lives. I'm not spoiled. Well at least I don't think so."

I leaned over and took her lips into mine. "Baby what are you thinking?"

"Brandon why would it matter to me how much money you have? I'm not your girlfriend."

I sat back then leaned forward slamming my fist on the dashboard. "That's enough of that shit Zoey! You're my fucking woman even if we don't tell people. You're mine!"

I paused for a moment. "Do you not want to be with me?"

She stared at me angrily.

I quickly captured her lips again as I slid my hand up her short dress feeling on her ass.

"Baby," I whispered against her cheek. "Do you love me?" I asked as I sucked on her neck.

"God yes," she mumbled.

"Listen baby," I said gazing into her eyes. "I will try to take it slow. I can't make any promises, alright?"

She shook her head yes against my hands. "This summer I'm taking you away."

Zoey smiled.

"Fuck I want you right now Zoey."

"Brandon we can't have sex in front of these people's mansion."

"Oh, this is my parent's house, it's cool."

"Brandon! I am definitely not having sex in front of your parent's house."

"Ok, just drive a little further down the street. Pull up to the gate," I instructed.

Once through the gate I instructed her to drive closer to the garage.

We walked toward the garage to enter the house.

"Brandon why did you pay my tuition?"

Shit, I thought.

"Baby, because I know how important it was for you to go back to school," I said looking over at her.

Zoey stopped walking. "Brandon you are trying to make it impossible for me to leave you. You are spoiling me, this is not taking it slow."

"Zoey I get the feeling you will leave when you're ready." I said not turning to look at her.

My heart plummeted to me feet. *Shit what if I was buying her to keep her with me? That's fucked up*, I thought.

I turned on my heels. "Listen, I'll stop buying you stuff."

She hesitated. "You don't really have to stop. Shit I don't want it to seem like I'm using you. I just don't know how to handle all of this. Truthfully it scares me."

There she goes capturing my heart again. I devoured her lips instantly making her hot and wet for me. I always know when she wants me. I can see it in her eyes. I smiled then grabbed her hand pulling her into the house.

"Mom!" I called out.

"Here I am Brandon dear," my mother said giving me a kiss on my cheek.

"Mom I would like you to meet Zoey."

"Zoey, it is so nice to meet you! I've heard so many great things about you," she said holding Zoey's hand in hers.

"Nice to meet you too, Mrs. Asher."

"Zoey join us in the family room for tea."

My mother took Zoey's arm in hers as they walked down the hall.

"Your home is beautiful," Zoey said as she looked around with her mouth open.

Zoey looked back at me giving me those I'm going to make you pay for holding out on me again looks. My mother and Zoey continued to talk. We all took a seat and in walked my Dad.

"Well hello Zoey," he said leaning down to give her a hug.

"Hello Mr. Asher it's very nice to meet you."

My father came over to give me a hug, too.

"So Zoey how do you like living in Boston?" asked Mr. Asher.

"I love it."

I've already versed my parents on what to ask Zoey. They have to keep it light or it will be another disaster like it was with Ryan and Melissa.

Our maid brought tea for everyone. My mother showed Zoey photos of me growing up while my Dad asked me how my residency was going.

"Dad, thanks for not making a scene at the hospital. I didn't want other doctors to think because I'm the chief's son, I should get special treatment."

"Not going to say it hasn't been hard, but you're welcome."

"Well Mom and Dad, we have to get going. I need to get fitted for my graduation suit and pick up my cap and gown early tomorrow."

I stood there holding Zoey's hand while we all said our goodbyes.

"Zoey we hope to see you at Brandon's graduation."

"Um," she said looking up at me with a confused look.

"Of course she will be there," I said squeezing her hand.

"Yes, I look forward to seeing you there," said Zoey.

CHAPTER TWELVE

BRANDON

When Zoey and I got back to my place I took a shower and she went to the kitchen to warm up the meal she prepared for me. That woman can cook her ass off!

After my shower I threw on a pair of navy blue basketball shorts and a white t-shirt. I sat at the dining room table to eat my meal.

"Thank you for this wonderful meal," I said pushing myself away from the table after I was done eating. I pulled Zoey into my arms.

"Are you ok with our unexpected meeting with my parents? I only ask because you were quiet on the way home."

"Yes, I'm fine! They are lovely people," she said moving my hair off my forehead.

"Thank you for agreeing to come to my graduation."

"You're welcome," she said kissing my forehead.

"I'm ready for dessert."

"Well I'm ready to be served," she smiled.

I pulled her dress over her head throwing it to the floor then I removed her bra exposing her breasts. They are nice and perky, just how I like them. I immediately took one of her breasts into my mouth. I held her by her waist in front of me while I continued sucking each of her nipples. Zoey ran her hands up the back of my head. I stood up and pulled her up into my arms allowing her to wrap her legs around my waist. She wrapped her arms around my neck and clamped her mouth down around mine then pushed her tongue into my mouth. She stopped kissing me to look down at me.

"Brandon do you realize we have spent two months together and have had sex every night?"

"Umm yeah I do. What's wrong with that?"

"Nothing I was thinking we have a pretty high sex drive," she said.

"Ha ha! Yeah we do." I walked her into the bedroom and laid her on the bed. "Wait is it too much? Did you want to take a break?"

"No I'm good. I think it will change once you have to study for your finals."

I stood at the foot of the bed taking my shirt and shorts off.

"You may be right because I usually don't have sex when its finals time. Although I've never had a sweet tasting piece of ass like yours so I don't know," I said pulling off her panties with my teeth.

"Brandon I missed you today."

"You know I would love to hear you say that forever."

"Oh Brandon that is so sweet."

"Come here baby," I demanded as I now laid at the top of the bed.

"What?" she asked.

"Come sit on my stomach."

She did as she was told. I scooted her bottom up onto my face.

"Brandon no! I've never done that before!" she pleaded trying to break free.

"Baby look at me. It's me. You don't have to hide from me. You know I'm not going to hurt you. If you don't like it, we can stop. Alright?"

"Ok," she said timidly.

"Hold onto the head board."

"Brandon I might crush you."

"No baby you won't. Trust me."

Zoey swallowed hard. "Ok."

I watched her scared face as she looked down at me. I held her legs tightly as I dipped my tongue deep inside of her. She still didn't know how to react to how she was feeling. I licked her ass and she closed her eyes. Zoey begin to moan as I pleased her. She instinctively tried to get up. I held her tighter as I ran my tongue back and forth down her slit. All her senses were heightened.

"Brandon," she said in a shaky voice. I sucked her little knob driving her completely insane.

She threw her head back, massaged one of her breasts as she held on tight to the head board. Her body jerked back against my mouth and I took my flat tongue and ran it from her ass to her clit. I circled my tongue around her clit just as she liked and she lost all control.

"Shiiit Brandon ba-by I'm cumming."

I sucked every part of her pussy and then she came hard just as I told her to cum.

I repeated myself. "Baby cum for me."

Zoey was out of breath from cumming so hard. "Oh I can't stop," she screamed at the top of her lungs.

After her second orgasm washed over her I let her go. She sat close to my dick then leaned over and kissed me. Before I could totally get my faculties together, she slid down on my dick. She bounced up and down on my dick making me sit up against the headboard. I pulled her closer to me, grabbed her ass pushing her up and down faster and faster making us both cum together. We laid there a minute to catch our breath.

"Come on let's take a bath," I said.

She laid perfectly in my arms in the tub. "I love you Brandon."

"I love you, too, Zoey."

Turned out Zoey was right, over the next few days I had so much going on I was too tired to have sex. Every morning she would wake me with a cup of coffee and a pep talk.

"Brandon school is almost over, you can do this! You are about to become a doctor."

While I studied at night Zoey partied. One night I received a call.

"Hello."

"Hello may I speak to Brandon?"

"Yes this is he."

"This is Zoey's friend Stacey."

I sat straight up.

"Hey Stacey what's going on?"

"I hate to bother you but Zoey is on a drinking bender again."

"What?!"

"Usually around this date Zoey drinks too much. She never told us why. Look is there any way you can come get her?"

"Of course! Text me the location of the club and I will be there.

"Ok bye," said Stacey.

I almost lost my head then I took a deep breath, threw on a suit and headed out.

I arrived at the club gave my keys to the valet to park my truck and walked to the front of the line.

"Hey Mr. Red Sox how are you doing tonight man?" the bouncer asked shaking my hand.

"Hey man I'm doing well."

"Go right in and let me know if you need anything," said the bouncer.

"Will do!" I replied.

I entered the club on a mission to find Zoey. It was so packed I could barely make it through the crowd. I went up to VIP and scanned my eyes across the crowd. I finally found her dancing on a table. I was pissed because the men around her had no respect for her. They didn't care she was drunk they just kept touching her ass. I pushed my way through the crowd until I reached her.

"Keep your fucking hands off her!" I shouted pushing one of the guys away.

"Fuck you man," the guy shouted.

Before I stepped to the guy his friend came in between us.

"We're good man we don't want any trouble just trying to stay chill."

"Alright I'm just here to get my girl," I stated.

I turned to Zoey grabbing the bottle of vodka out of her hand.

"Baby, look at me, we need to leave."

"Brandon- my Brandon," she slurred wrapping her arms around my neck.

I took my jacket off placing it over Zoey to cover her short puffy skirt. She raised her hand in the sky. "My Billionaire boyfriend is here to rescue me!" she shouted.

I didn't say a word as I noticed people taking my picture and typing messages on their phones.

"Brandon!" Stacey yelled out.

"Stacey why didn't you stay with Zoey?" I beseeched.

"When she's like this she asks to be left alone. We just check on her throughout the night then come and get her when it's time to leave. I've never seen her this bad off," admitted Stacey.

"Do you need me to take you home?" I asked shouting over the music.

"No my girl Kamren is here, we're leaving later."

"Text me when you both get home," I demanded holding Zoey close to me.

"Alright," said Stacey.

Zoey broke away from my grasp and started dancing again.

"Brandon baby I told you I can't be saved. You need to let me go."

I am past pissed at this point. I picked Zoey up, threw her across my shoulder, and swiftly made my way to the exit.

"Stay cool," said the Bouncer.

"You too, man."

I sat Zoey in the passenger seat and buckled her in. When I climbed into the driver's seat I wanted to ask her what's going on, but I didn't. I started driving down the street.

"I want to go home," slurred Zoey.

"Alright we will be there soon."

"No Brandon, my apartment."

"Ok."

We arrived at her apartment a short time later. I carried her to her apartment door, unlocked it then stood her on her feet.

"Goodnight Zoey."'

"Brandon please don't leave me," she cried.

"Zoey, baby of course not, I'll stay."

It was probably wrong of me to never ask her if she wanted us to stay at her place sometimes.

We stood in the middle of Zoey's bedroom. She fell into my arms sinking her tear stained face into my chest.

"Baby you don't have to do this alone anymore," I assured her.

Zoey didn't respond. I pulled her chin up so she could look into my eyes and understand that what I was saying was true.

"Zoey we are a team. You can trust me. Just know I'm your rock. I will stand right here with you. We will weather this storm together. No matter how long it takes. Zoey, even if it's so fucked up that I give you the side eye we can still work through it. But you gotta let me in."

"Brandon how do you expect me to get past my mother never talking to me again for something that wasn't my fault entirely?" she asked walking over to window. She leaned her head against the windowpane staring out into the night. "It wasn't all on me. Shit even if it was I was a teenager. I think I'm going to be sick," she replied stumbling to the bathroom.

She dropped to her knees in front of the toilet, leaned over releasing all of the contents from her stomach. I held her hair until she was finished. I then wet a towel and wiped her face and mouth. I picked her up and carried her to bed, laid her down and removed her clothes leaving her in only her panties. What can I say I love looking at her breasts. I undressed down to my boxers and climbed into the bed with her, pulling her into my arms. I watched her sleep. *I need to meet her mother. I wanted to see if there was any way they could reconcile*, I thought.

CHAPTER THIRTEEN

BRANDON

The next day I informed Zoey I had a study group later that night. "Are you coming back home with me?" Zoey peeked around the shower curtain.

"Brandon I don't want to disturb your studies. Trust me I would only be a distraction," she said biting her lip. I stood in the doorway dressed in my suit looking into her big beautiful brown eyes.

"Baby let me be the judge of that," I said as I walked over to kiss her perfect lips.

"I love you baby."

She batted her long lashes. "I love you too, Brandon. I will possibly see you later."

I smiled back. "See you later sweetheart."

Later that afternoon my study group partners arrived.

"Hey my man Ted. What's happening brother."

"Just ready to graduate!" exclaimed Ted.

"Shit you're telling me!" I stated.

Stan, Sandy, and Rob arrived shortly after.

"Let's get started guys anyone want something to drink?" I asked.

"I'll take a bottle of water," said Sandy.

"Red bull guys?" I asked.

"Yes please!" the guys responded.

I passed out everyone's drinks as I sat down on the couch next to Sandy.

"Hey man where have you been? You haven't been to the Frat house in a long time," asked Rob.

"I've been hanging out with my friend Zoey," I responded smiling.

"Damn man it looks like someone is whipped! Shit what is it like?" asked Rob.

"What?" I asked.

"Fucking one woman. That is something you just don't do," confirmed Rob.

I ran my hand down the back of my hair and glanced over at Sandy. It's harder than I thought. Sitting next to a woman I was once intimate with talking about the love of my life. When I first arrived at college I was fucking every beautiful chick I could find. I found if I fucked the same chick to many times she got attached, so I developed a rule after freshman year not to fuck the same woman more than four times. Ryan and I were living in the dorms at the time so I would always bring girls there. My system was to fuck three girls a semester. I would have sex with one woman in September, one in October, and then one in November.

I was very honest I let them know I wasn't looking for anything serious I only wanted to play. Sometimes it didn't matter how blunt I was, women would still try to see me regularly. And no, I wasn't fucking any of them every day, I would limit it. A girl could come over and suck my dick or we would fuck. I didn't have sex close to mid-terms or finals. Women would still get upset when I wouldn't have sex with them after a month's time. I wasn't a total dick, I always made sure women got their rocks off. Shit, maybe I shouldn't have made them cum, then they probably wouldn't have wanted to come back for more.

Once I got into the medical program, I moved off campus into a condo. I enhanced my system. I started to fuck women at the Frat house. I wanted more from Zoey so I brought her back to my place. She was different to me, I wanted to learn her body, something I never cared to do before. Shit, I got off track thinking about Zoey, she invades my thoughts every time. I better get her off my mind before my dick gets hard. I didn't really bring women back to my apartment if I could help it. Just this year I got a little relaxed and brought Sandy back to my place. I remember the last encounter I had with Sandy was different.

Sandy met me at my Condo after classes.

"Hello Sandy how was class?" I asked walking over to unlock my door.

"They were alright I only went to two today," she replied.

We sat on the couch to study, after we were done we went to my bedroom.

Sandy pulled my t-shirt over my head immediately and started licking my nipples. She got on her knees unbuckled my pants, then dropped to the floor and started sucking my dick. Sandy did a good job, probably another reason she stayed around so long. I pulled her up then laid her in the middle of the bed. I peeled her clothes off, leaned over her kissing her neck down to her breast. I licked her nipples while I slid my finger in and out her pussy. I reached for a condom and rolled it down my staff. I kissed her stomach then licked her belly button. She ran her fingers threw my hair then started pushing me head down to her pussy. I kissed each thigh, sat up and thrust inside her hard.

"Oh yeah Brandon," she moaned.

I flipped her over to fuck her from behind. I slammed into her pussy each time. She begged for more. She doesn't look like it but she's a very dirty talker.

"Fuck my pussy harder," she screamed.

"That's it yes, yes I'm cumming!" she screamed.

"Yeah give me that pussy girl! Shit!" I yelled as I came.

I fell down on the bed beside her, kissed her lips, and laid there with her in my arms.

"Brandon do you ever see more for us? We work well together in a lot of ways. I think we could work better together in a relationship."

"Sandy I'm not looking for anything serious right now, just trying to graduate."

"Oh ok cool," she said.

"Sorry Sandy, I know our sex together can be pretty intense but we agreed that this is all it would be."

Sandy was the last woman I had sex with before Zoey. This afternoon I've noticed Sandy has been a little quiet, probably because I disrupted my system. I digressed, I liked Sandy but not enough to make her my woman.

Ted interrupted my thoughts. "Brandon when did you start fucking black chicks?" Ted inquired.

"I hadn't before Zoey, she is the first black woman I've ever been with."

"Dude you're whipped! You're in the newspaper together. There's a picture of the two of you on the Jumbo Tron at a Red Sox game. Does she know you're Mr. Red Sox and that you're expected to carry on family tradition by taking on some of the players as patients once you become a doctor?" Ted quizzed.

"She knows enough. She knows about my family history and she knows I will be a billionaire in four years."

"Brandon, technically you already are because you come from a family of billionaires."

"Zoey is different she doesn't want my money or a relationship. I'm the one trying to get her to be in a relationship but she won't do it."

I don't look over at Sandy because I can feel that she is angry with me. Don't get me wrong, Sandy is beautiful. She has long blonde hair, blue eyes, stays in shape and about 5'7" in height. She is the recommended woman for me by society, but I don't want that. I want my beautiful mocha woman who makes love to me like there is no tomorrow, and who I have the best time with. I know I have to be honest with myself, I don't know if Zoey will stick around and the thought makes me sick to my stomach.

"Ted I guess you're right. I'm a little whipped."

"So do we get to meet the great Zoey?" asked Sandy.

"I don't know if she's coming over or not."

Just as I say those words, I hear a key turning in the lock. Damn these guys are going to let me have it.

"Who is that? I thought Ryan moved out?" asked Stan.

"It's Zoey!"

"Man you really are whipped," stated Ted.

I jumped up from the couch to greet Zoey. When she entered the condo, my dick got hard. Zoey looked absolutely beautiful. She never wears a lot of makeup, but she had on a face full today. She wore her hair pressed, her tresses fell to the middle of her back. I stared at her in disbelief. She's wearing a beige trench coat and the purple bottom stilettos I had custom made for her.

"Brandon why are you staring at me like that aren't you going to introduce me to your friends?" she asked closing the door behind her.

Why did this woman do this to me? I looked her up and down then grabbed her hand pulling her toward my bedroom.

"I will be right back!" I said to my guests.

I closed the door behind us and I took a seat on the bed. I looked up at her. "What are you doing?"

"You said I wouldn't be a distraction," she affirmed.

"Yeah, I lied."

I untied the trench coat revealing her black bra and panties with purple trim. Zoey noticed my dick was so hard. She dropped the coat to the floor then fell to her knees. She unleashed my manhood from my pants.

"Don't say a word Brandon. I want to thank you for yesterday and I wanted to release some of your stress for finals."

She took my dick into her mouth in a flash. She held onto my thighs as she continued sucking. She licked my staff up and down then around the head. I rubbed her hair and started confessing shit to her again. I mean shit, she had me by the balls, literally. She played with my balls while she sucked my dick.

"Zoey shit you got my heart. I love you! Damn I love you!"

"Zoey I'm about to cum," I moaned.

Zoey ran her hand up and down my dick and sucked faster bobbing her head up and down, repeatedly until I exploded into her mouth.

"Damn baby that was fucking amazing," I groaned out.

Zoey just smiled at me.

"Baby can you leave on the bra and panties for later? I need you to put on some clothes though. I don't need my friends imaging what my woman looks like under a trench coat," I said kissing each of her breasts.

"Alright I will put on something else," she said walking over to the closet.

She stood in the walk in closet looking for an outfit. I walked up behind her, slid my hand down in her panties circling her clit with just one finger.

Her head rest against my chest.

"You're a bad girl Zoey Asher! After a stunt like that you will have to be my wife."

I walked around in front of her and swept my lips across hers bringing her tongue into my mouth. I caressed her face.

"Baby I have to get back out there before they think we are in here having sex. Oh, before I go I left out a critical fact about one of the members of my study group. I was sleeping with Sandy right before I met you. She maybe a little bitter that her time was cut short with me because I met you and I stopped seeing her. I have always studied with her and I should have talked her beforehand and told her we can't study together."

Zoey backed me up against the wall. "Is she going to be my first victim?" she asked sourly.

"Baby she means nothing to me."

"Brandon, I'm not mad. It just reminds me of how all those women whispered and said mean shit about me at the Frat party," she said shrugging her shoulders.

"Zoey why did you wait so long to tell me?"

"Brandon, it doesn't matter, we're here now, right?"

"Baby it does matter to me."

"Brandon that's what I love about you. How you care for me."

"Hey, get back out there for they seriously think we're having sex," she giggled.

"Alright, but this isn't over," I confirmed.

I walked out the room and sat on the couch. My friends stared at me.

"What?!" I said.

"Dude you were moaning like a little bitch," said Stan laughing.

"Zoey you got my heart! I love you," they guys all mocked me.

"Man you never mentioned you were in love. Wait how is that? You haven't even known her that long," said Rob.

"I can't explain it, but I knew it the first night I met her that she was the woman I wanted to be with for the rest of my life."

"Sandy can I talk to you for a minute?"

"Sure," she replied.

I walked over and slid open the sliding door to my balcony. I let her walk out on the balcony first then I closed the door behind us.

"Sandy I believe I owe you an apology. I'm sorry for never talking to you about Zoey until now. I get what we had wasn't serious but I still consider you a friend and if we are going to continue to study together I need you to know I don't fuck around anymore with any woman. I am with Zoey now."

"Well that is obvious," she said in a bitter tone.

"Brandon, I want you to know it's kind of weird how you are around intelligent women every day at Harvard, and you fall in love with a bar worker."

"How the fuck do you know what she does for a living? Were you spying on her?

Sandy paused. "I was curious. I wanted to know what was so special about her. Why you chose her over me," she said looking down at the floor.

"Sandy, I'm sorry if I hurt you, but I didn't ever see a relationship developing between us. It was only sex." I moved closer to her looking her in the eye. "I don't want to find out that you are following her or saying shit to her. Do not cross me Sandy! I made my decision. I wouldn't care if she worked at a fucking hot dog stand on the corner, she is who I choose! If you have a problem with her you can leave right now," I spewed pointing to the door.

"Brandon, I don't want to lose our friendship over a woman. I apologize for acting like a jealous girl. Let's get back to our studies," she said smiling.

CHAPTER FOURTEEN
ZOEY

I was in the kitchen looking through the cabinets for something to cook when I noticed Brandon and Sandy walking in from the balcony. I take it he told her she was no longer a part of his sex escapades, but of course I would be sure to inquire. I told the guys I was going to whip up something to eat. Looks like I need to go to the store to buy my ingredients.

Brandon made sure I always had access to cash. He deposited money into my checking and savings account. He deposited three times my salaries at both my old jobs for the year. I told him that was not necessary but he told me he wanted to make sure I was taken care of and that he didn't want me working my jobs anymore. I told him I wasn't going to quit. He wasn't too happy about that. He asked me if I could work for him part time at one of his three charity organizations. I agreed so I guess he got what he wanted. He said he has peace of mind knowing I'm safe.

He preferred I take money out of the safe if I needed to do miscellaneous things like go grocery shopping. If I needed to purchase large items, I could use his credit cards. Today I wanted to be spontaneous so I stopped into a couple of stores to buy the lingerie and Trench coat. When Brandon took me shopping, he told the manager at each store to add me to his accounts so I could buy what I wanted when I wanted. I was flabbergasted when this took place. I mean why did he do that? I felt he was trying to keep me to ensure I didn't leave him. He even paid for my tuition for the entire school year. Shit, matter fact I know he was trying to keep me. He did that in hopes that I wouldn't leave.

He was so caring the other night asking me how I felt after meeting his parents. I admit I was a little taken aback and a little overwhelmed. His mom and dad were so nice to me, I felt comfortable around them. I went from having nothing to having everything in a just a couple of months. The only reason I got behind in my studies was because of the drinking and depression. I have been less depressed since I've been with Brandon than I have been in ten years. Well, we can talk about the rest in a little while, first I have something up my sleeve.

"So I am happy to cook for y'all but I have to run to the store. Sandy would you like to come with?"

If you could see all of the red faces in the room, oh what a treat.

"Yes, sure!" replied Sandy.

She and I walked swiftly towards the door.

"Zoey," Brandon said walking in close proximity.

"Baby! What are you doing?" he asked grabbing my hips placing his forehead against mine.

I rubbed his chest while looking into his eyes. "Baby, its ok I'm a big girl," I said gently kissing his lips.

He looked at me like I was a porcelain doll that needed protecting.

"We will be back soon," I confirmed.

Sandy and I climbed into Brandon's Range Rover and I made my way in the direction of the grocery store. "So Sandy how's Harvard medical school treating you?"

"Well. How's Boston University treating you?" asked Sandy.

"Oh you looked me up. Seems like Ms. Harvard was intimidated by little old Ms. Boston," I snickered.

"Cut the shit, we both know what you are, a money grubbing two-bit tramp. Brandon is the only one so deep in your pussy he can't see the truth!"

"Yup, deep all the time. I can tell Brandon's the giving type and would not ever have sex with a woman unless he made her cum. So how many times did he make you cum in one night?"

Sandy folded her arms defensively, "I wouldn't dignify that with an answer!"

"Hum, well let me see, how's about I over share. Just thinking about Brandon right now makes me want to cum."

"You're sick!" Sandy spit out.

"Maybe just little," I teased.

"No but seriously the first night I went back to his condo I had every intention of a one-night stand, but I guess you ladies weren't doing your job. because he had to have me again and again. Each time he made me cum. He said he wanted to learn all of my cum faces. I thought that was cute and it worked for me. I figured he used it on all the women. This man is so addicted to licking my pussy, I found myself having to pull him up for air. I see why you ladies are so taken by him," I said flashing my devilish grin.

I parked the truck near the entrance of the supermarket. "Well let's hurry up and get those ingredients. You know what they say, the way to man's heart is through his stomach."

I knew I had got under med girl's skin but I didn't give a shit. Remember what I told Brandon, I don't want him fucking another woman because I would be willing to kill a bitch. Needless to say I am hard at work driving home to this Bitch not to fuck with my territory. I rushed through the store throwing needed food items into my cart.

"You do know you're just the new flavor in Brandon's bowl. He's never been with a black woman and he just wanted to see what it was like for a while."

"You may be right," I said as I stopped in the middle of the aisle to look at her. "I will continue to make love to him or fuck his brains out, whichever he prefers."

On our drive back I decided to ask a few more questions. "Sandy how much longer do you think he will keep me around? Let's see, I have been here for two months that is his magic number right? He's got to send me on my way soon. That's why he gave me his truck to drive, gave me a key to his condo, he asked me to stay over every night. He gets upset if and when I go home, he hired me as CEO of his charity, and last but not least, I met his parents the other day. Yeah I would say I will definitely be on my way soon," I smirked again.

"Look here you little slut! Brandon can't see you're nothing more than a fake bitch chasing after his money and status. If you think we will let you come here and steal him from us. You have another thing coming!" she spit out.

"Well looks like it's your last night around Brandon," I spewed with fury.

I pulled into Brandon's parking space at his condo. "Listen Sandy, I don't like you and you don't like me but let's get through tonight for Brandon."

Sandy sat there a minute. "Fine for Brandon."

There was dead silence when we walked through the door. The guys stared at us.

"Who's hungry?" I asked.

"Me," said Stan.

"Well let me get started on dinner," I stated.

Sandy sat down on the couch next to Brandon. Brandon looked at her then me in a curious manner. I broke our stare and started preparing the lasagna for dinner and peach cobbler for dessert.

I didn't bother Brandon while he studied. I kept to myself. I couldn't help to toss around all the shit that Sandy bitch had to say about me. Rich women always call women they feel are beneath them 'gold digging sluts'. That is a jealous woman's first line of defense. A woman of her stature believes the only reason a rich white man would be with a black woman is because she's an experiment. I know that is not true. I touch my lips as I think back to our first kiss. Brandon entered the kitchen breaking my train of thought.

"Are you ok? Do you need any help?"

Brandon stood behind me wrapping his arms around my waist, kissing the top of my head and leaning his manhood into my back. That shit drove me crazy.

"No," I replied as I continued to press the edges of the pie crust.

I remembered not to moan. My eyes met Ted's as I peered out into the living room.

"Brandon stop! First of all, you're making me hot, second your friends are watching us."

"Fine I will stop for now, but later I'm going to make you scream my name."

I don't say anything but my flush face tells it all. Brandon smiled at me when he returned to the couch. Once dessert was complete I sat the lasagna and peach cobbler in the middle of the dining room table. I made sure I had enough place settings for everyone.

"Dinner is served."

Once everyone took their place I walked around the table serving everyone a portion of lasagna.

"Zoey dinner smells delicious! Who taught you how to cook?" Stan asked.

I looked over at Brandon's nervous face. "My grandmother. You can't be from the south and not know how to cook. Every summer I sat in my grandmother's kitchen cooking new dishes."

"I hope you all enjoy," I said as I took my seat at the head of the table across from Brandon.

I was proud of myself. For the first time I didn't run. I figured out a way to answer the questions without freaking out. I enjoyed listening to Brandon's friends share stories about him. Sandy didn't say anything to me other than dinner was delicious. Ted insisted on helping me clear the table.

"Zoey, thanks for taking care of my friend. You are like a breath of fresh air for him. As long as I've known Brandon he's wanted a girlfriend. However, my buddy can be picky. Secretly I think what he was looking for was a woman with some spunk who wouldn't take his shit. Women can be too accommodating sometimes and it becomes an instant turn off to men."

"Thanks Ted, I appreciate the kind words," I exclaimed as I took a stack of dirty plates from his hands and placed them in the sink.

Once everyone was gone Brandon helped me load the dishwasher then he ran me a bath. While I soaked in the tub Brandon continued studying. I got out of the tub, oiled my body down, and put on the black bra and panties with pink trim. I poured myself a glass of red wine and retired to my favorite chair in front of the large picture window. I finally felt a sense of peace. I was considering moving on with the next chapter in my life; Brandon. If I could persuade him not to have kids, we would be perfect together.

Brandon quietly walked over to me and sat on his knees at my feet.

"Baby are you ok?"

"Yes," I replied marveling in his eyes.

He reached for my glass of wine and took a large sip.

"Um I see you bought two lingerie sets. Stand up."

I stood and he took my hand twirling me around until my ass was in his face.

"Damn you're beautiful," he whispered as he placed both of his large hands on one of my ass cheeks.

He pulled my panties down just a bit and opened his mouth against my skin taking a portion of my ass into his mouth. This sent shivers up my spine. He did this to both sides of my ass. He slid his finger down the slit of my panties against my pussy.

"Bend over," he commanded.

He slid my wet panties down my thighs until they hit the floor. He helped me step out of my panties one leg at a time.

"Spread your legs baby."

I held on to the chair cushion as Brandon gently pried my lips apart. He wasted no time sucking my clit. He twirled his tongue around my clit sending my juices right into his mouth. He then slid his tongue slowly within each of my folds to my ass and back to my clit.

"Brandon, baby please stop I can't hold myself up!"

"I'm in love with your pussy baby," he groaned as he held my lower body in his arms.

"I got you, baby," he murmured against my pussy.

Brandon pushed his tongue in and out of me fast while he played with my clit.

"Oh God," I moaned loudly as I came again and again.

With one swift move he turned my body around planting me in the chair and placed my legs over his shoulders. He continued on his quest to make me cum some more. Brandon ran the flat part of his tongue from my ass to my clit sending my body into shiver attacks. Brandon didn't let up assaulting my body. He stopped only to remove his clothes.

He looked into my eyes, "Baby are you going to cum for me again?"

I didn't answer him. He kissed my thigh then slid his finger in and out of me while he made his way up to my breasts. Brandon took one of my nipples in his mouth and bit down as he slammed into me. I swear I saw stars on impact.

"Fuck you feel good!" he yelled. Brandon devoured my lips as he pulled me by my ass towards him stroking back and forth.

"Brandon," I cried against his lips.

"Promise you won't leave me Zoey."

I couldn't respond. All I could do was caress his face as I cried. The tears flowed down my cheeks like a stream. I closed my eyes laying my head against his shoulder. Brandon stood us up as my legs instinctively wrapped around his waist. He walked over to closest wall pressing my back firmly against it. He swiped his large hand softly across my face making the tears disappear.

I gently kissed his lips. "Brandon, I don't want to leave you but it's selfish of me to stay, and I can't give you the family you want."

"I promise I want nothing more than to be with you forever but I can-."

Brandon slammed his lips into mine. "Zoey you're my family now and forever."

He carried me into the bedroom and gently laid me down while he remained inside me.

He hovered over me while his eyes peered into my soul as we made love. I ran my fingers across Brandon's abs back up to his face. "I'm deeply in love with you Brandon Christopher Asher II."

He smiled at me before taking my lips into his. He thrust deep inside me as he came. Brandon rested his face on the side of my neck. I dropped my legs down at his sides. Brandon swiftly made his way out the bed not saying a word. He walked into the bathroom and started taking a shower. I could tell I tore out a piece of his heart. I lay in the bed biting my nails. I should be flattered that this wonderful man wants to have a family with me. Unfortunately, I feel indifferent, do I stay or go? I need to speak to my psychiatrist again, I thought as laid back down and dosed off.

CHAPTER FIFTEEN

BRANDON

I stood over Zoey watching her sleep while I dried my hair. I love this woman with everything in me. I ripped the towel from my waist and got in the bed pulling her into my arms. I laid my lips upon the top of her head.

"Zoey I love you. I hate that you don't want to have a family with me. God baby, I want so much for you to bear my children. I want a beautiful baby girl who looks just like you. Baby why won't you give me that? I want nothing but happiness for us. If you won't bear my children it will just be you and I forever," I revealed as a single tear rolled down my cheek.

In the morning I rushed around my bedroom getting ready for class. I have to take my last final today and tomorrow my last exam to become a doctor.

"Brandon do you need me to help you do anything?" she asked yawning.

"No don't worry about it beautiful," I said leaning over to kiss her lips.

"We are going out to dinner tonight to celebrate me finishing school. I'm driving the Range today. I'll leave the keys to the Porsche on the counter ok?"

"Alright."

"I love you baby, bye," I said.

"Bye."

Later that afternoon I sat around the Frat house waiting for my friends to arrive.

"Yeah B dawg we did it! Med school is officially over!" shouted Ted as he walked through the door with some of our friends.

We gathered around the bar. I poured everyone a shot of Tequila.

"Let's toast to finals being over, taking our last exam tomorrow to become doctors, and finally graduating from Harvard! Whoa!" I screamed as we clank our shoot glasses together.

"Let's toast to Brandon finally finding the one!" said Rob.

"Thanks man," I replied.

"You're a lucky man, she can cook her ass off," Ted conveyed.

I chuckled.

"I never seen you look at a woman like that and I have known you since we arrived at Harvard," Stan said.

"Yeah, she is the one," I replied.

"A toast to Zoey! The great B dawg has officially retired."

"Here, Here!" we bellowed one by one.

Hell what could I say? It was true, I met my match. I wasn't interested in any other woman but Zoey. I looked back on our time spent together. Sure, we fight and argue but we're not like most couples. We don't argue about where we are going to dinner. We argue about her having the girlfriend title. I still cringe just thinking about it. It's so fucked up to introduce Zoey as my friend when she is clearly my girlfriend. Shit, your friend doesn't share the same bed, take showers with you, tell you she loves you forever and doesn't want anyone else to be with you, or make love to you every single night. No, that is most definitely a girlfriend. I hate that I couldn't tell Zoey how I felt while she was awake for fear that she would leave me. I have to talk to her mother, I'm tired of this shit I need her to open up to me. I am also more than willing to go to counseling so we can move forward. I'm willing to do anything to bring her closer. I want my babies to come from her, period, I thought.

After drinks at the Frat house with my friends I needed some time to myself. I went for drinks at my favorite bar in Boston. My life with Zoey is bitter sweet.

"Hey Josh I'll have another," I yell to the bartender at the other end of the bar.

Josh grabbed the top shelf scotch from the shelf then poured it into a glass. I quickly drank it down. I slammed the glass down. "Hit me again."

"Is everything ok?" asked Josh.

"Yeah,yeah. Here's to me graduating from Harvard University!" I said as I raised my glass.

Josh drank a shot with me. My phone rang.

"Hey baby what's up?" I asked as I ran my hand through my hair.

"Brandon where are you?" quizzed Zoey.

"I'm at Legal Crossing."

"I'll be there soon," said Zoey before she hung up.

"Josh can you reserve a booth for me please?"

"Sure thing Brandon."

One thing about my affiliation with the Red Sox is that everyone knows me. Every bar I go to, restaurant or club wherever; if you've been to Fenway Park, you know my family.

I looked up from my glass to see Zoey standing next to me. "Zoeeey!" I said kissing her forehead.

"Hey everybody it's my girlfriend Zoey!" I said turning to the patrons. I turned back only to see Zoey's angry face staring back at me.

"I'm sorry my friend."

"Brandon what is the meaning of this?" she asked still standing close to me.

"What I can't have a drink after finishing finals?" I asked.

"So you forgot you made dinner plans with me," said Zoey.

"Shit I'm sorry Zoey. The day got away from me."

"Josh which booth?"

"Near the window in the corner," he replied.

"Thanks man."

I grabbed Zoey's hand and led her to the booth.

"Baby you look beautiful tonight," I told her as I kissed her cheek.

Zoey wore her hair in big spiral curls, a red form fitted dress, spaghetti straps with the back out and black and beige strappy stilettos. That dress hugged every curve on her body just right. Let's just say, when we walked to our table every man was looking at my woman.

I sat there in silence rubbing her hand while she scrolled down the menu with her free hand.

"Good evening Mr. Asher, may I take your order?"

"Zoey are you ready to order?"

"Yes I will have a salad with Balsamic vinegar dressing and chicken breast with mashed potatoes and asparagus."

"I will have porterhouse steak with a baked potato and broccoli. Also, bring us a bottle of Pellegrino, please. Thank you."

"Brandon what's the matter?" asked Zoey.

"Everything is better now that you are here," I said kissing her neck.

"I want you Zoey," I stated looking into her eyes.

Zoey smiled, caressed my face, and whispered in my ear, "I'm wet for you right now."

"I'm going to eat my dinner before I fuck your brains out. I need to eat to keep up my strength," I said smiling.

"My graduation ceremony and party is Tuesday of next week. I will be introducing you going forward as my girlfriend. I don't want you fussing with me about how you're not that, because you are, period". I leaned forward and looked into her worried eyes. "Listen, there's no harm in being loved in every way."

I pressed my lips against hers then pushed my tongue past her lips intertwining our tongues in a sacred dance. I released her lips only to turn my attention to the waitress who had just arrived with our food.

"Thank you," I responded to the waitress who looked almost more flustered then Zoey as she walked away.

"Baby are you ok?"

"Yes."

I reached into my blazer pocket and pulled out a ring box.

Zoey's eyes were big as saucers. "Zoey calm down it's just a promise ring."

I removed the custom 5-carat pink and platinum diamond ring from the ring box and slipped it on to the fourth finger on her right hand.

She admired the ring placing her hand up to the light. "What do I say if someone asks me about the ring?"

"Zoey, whatever you want to tell them. You can say my man bought me a promise ring or you can say it's just a ring."

Zoey clutched my face with both hands stared into my eyes then pressed her lips against mine. "Brandon I don't deserve you."

"Baby, I don't deserve you. You are kind, loving, and the perfect woman for me."

I called a car service I use when I've had too much to drink. They will pick up my truck, the Porsche and send a car service to pick us up.

"A car service will be here in fifteen minutes to take us home."

"How do you like your new job?" I asked as I paid the bill then led her out of the door of the restaurant.

"Brandon, there is so much work to do at Asher Charities. I have to make myself leave by 6 p.m."

"Zoey, you are the boss, so you need to leave around 6 p.m. at the latest." I pulled her into my arms and looked down at her. "You don't want me to come to your office and let everyone know you're being a bad girl. Do you?"

"Well actually I do want you to come to my office and have your way with me," she giggled.

The driver pulled up, walked around, and opened the rear passenger door for us. Zoey slid across the seat and I sat next to her.

"You have the address, correct?"

"Yes sir, we thank you for riding with 'Plush Services'!" said the driver."

"You're welcome," I replied rolling up the partition.

I laid Zoey down across the seat, removed her panties slid her dress up her thighs, and dove right into her pussy. I licked her hole in a circular motion.

"Brandon, oh God, oh shit!" she screamed at the top of her lungs while she pulled at my blazer then my hair. I think she was trying to stop me, I'm not sure. I stretched my hand trying to cover her mouth but I couldn't because she had arched her back pressing her pussy deeper into my face. I kissed her thirsty hole, licked in between her folds, and then sucked her clit until she came a second time.

Zoey sat up quick; curled up into the corner of the seat. Her eyes we're closed and she was crying.

"Zoey what's wrong?" I quizzed trying to pull her towards me.

I noticed the car stopped.

I cracked the window to see if we were in front of my condo. I hit the intercom button. "Give us a minute."

"Take your time, sir."

Zoey was still crying uncontrollably. I tried pulling her close to me but she pushed me away.

"Don't touch me anymore," she cried.

"Zoey baby! Please look at me!" I pleaded holding her face firmly in my hands. "Zoey, baby please talk to me! Open your eyes and look at me! It's Brandon."

The minute I said that, she opened her eyes. It was as if something clicked in her head.

She looked me up and down. "Brandon!" she said with a sigh of relief. She fell into my arms nuzzled into my chest rubbing my soak and wet beard.

"I'm here, baby. You don't have to do this alone," I said caressing her hair.

"We will discuss this later. We can't move on in our relationship until we do."

I was a fool for thinking we could. It appeared as if someone was attacking her. I wondered if someone harmed her. I just don't know. Whatever it was she and I will get through it. I carried Zoey up to my condo. I laid her down on the bed so she could rest. I shed my clothes putting them into the hamper, then walked into the bathroom to do my nightly ritual. I was brushing my teeth when I noticed Zoey walk in, pick up her toothbrush and join me.

"I'm going to run you a bath."

"Brandon only if you will join me."

"Of course baby." I pulled Zoey into my arms giving her a big hug.

We sat in the tub in silence just enjoying the hot bath.

Zoey turned around, straddled me, and pushed her tongue into my mouth.

"I need to feel you inside of me," she whispered in my ear.

I picked Zoey up and eased her down on my dick. I grabbed her right breast, licked around her areola, and sucked each nipple hard driving Zoey insane. She rested her hands on the back of the tub pushing herself up and down my dick. I caressed her from her neck down to her ass. I slowly pushed my finger into her ass sending her orgasm over the edge. I watched her as she closed her eyes and bit her lower lip. "Zoey baby look at me. I love you, sweetheart don't ever forget that. I need you too, baby."

I gripped Zoey's ass tight as I bit down on her neck, pounding away at her pussy. I pushed my dick deep inside her fast, repeatedly, until we came together.

After we got dressed for bed, we slid under the sheets, and I pulled Zoey into my arms intertwining our fingers.

"Brandon. What's going to happen when our two months are up?"

"Zoey are you serious?" I asked in disbelief.

"Yes that is your limit to keep a woman."

"Zoey I was never in a relationship with any of those women it was just sex. Baby what you and I have together is different. If I didn't think you would run from me this promise ring would have been an engagement ring," I confirmed picking up her hand.

"Sweetheart there is no one else but you. I know you're afraid to bring children into this world. However, I want us to sit down with your psychiatrist and see how we can help you move past that fear. You're safe with me."

"Brandon! You are pushing it."

"Baby I understand, but I know how I see our future."

"Zoey are you going to leave me?"

She didn't respond.

"I want you to know I want all of you!"

"Brandon I want us to sit down after you've graduated and talk about what happened to me."

She didn't answer my question about leaving me, but for the first time she's willing to share her past. I feel that is a step in the right direction.

CHAPTER SIXTEEN

ZOEY

I woke up to the morning light peeking through the drapes. I scurried to the kitchen to make Brandon's breakfast. *Brandon had finally finished his finals for school yesterday. Today is huge for Brandon. The test he takes today will determine if he becomes a doctor or not. I am so proud of him,* I thought, smiling.

I hate that I blacked out on Brandon last night. Shit he was licking my pussy so good; it was amazing. I hate that Martin infiltrated my thoughts. I thought back to when I had sex with him. I imagined myself fighting him off me. I wish I had gone to my grandmother when he first raped me. My psychiatrist told me that's what it was, rape. She said he groomed me from the age of thirteen to trust him so that when he propositioned me I would be a willing participant. My skin crawled at the thought of him on top of me. I can't believe I thought I was in love with him.

"Good morning, baby!" I jumped when Brandon kissed my neck and rubbed my arms. The plate of bacon I was holding flew all over the floor.

"Oh my God. I'm so sorry!" I fell to my knees and started picking up the broken plate pieces.

Brandon got down on his knees and helped me pick everything up. The tears poured down my cheeks. Brandon looked at me with wide eyes.

"Come here sweetheart, have a seat," he said.

Brandon grabbed some Kleenex and wiped my face. "Zoey it's getting worse."

"Brandon this is why I shouldn't be in a relationship. The memories are resurfacing."

"I can reschedule my test," he said.

I looked at him with angry eyes. "You will do no such thing," I said poking him in his chest.

"I will schedule an appointment for Thursday of next week for us to see my psychiatrist. I will be just fine as long as I know I have you by my side," I said smiling.

He in turn smiled back at me.

"Now let me make you another plate."

While Brandon was taking his test, I got fitted for two dresses, one dress for his graduation and one for his graduation cocktail party. *Rich people. Regular people just had a party, received gifts, danced, and ate. Rich people turned a graduation party into a networking event,* I thought shaking my head.

I have a few more outfits to buy for our three-month excursion. Brandon is off for the summer. He said he had been planning this trip for a long time. He was going with his friends. However, he told them he wanted to spend most of his time with me on the trip and we would meet up with them for dinner sometimes.

Who knew I would get my happily ever after. Maybe this was God's way of making up for the tragedy that happened to me. When I met Brandon I just thought he was a regular guy. I didn't believe he was a billionaire until he showed me the letter that said one billion dollars would be deposited into his checking account when he turned thirty years old. He already had millions in his accounts. When Brandon started college he received his first trust fund payout of $500,000. At the age of twenty-five he received a second payout of two million dollars. I know you are probably thinking why wouldn't I jump at the chance to be with a billionaire. Instead I fight him at every turn. It's not about the money. It is about this man's patience with me that keeps me grounded by his side.

∞

Brandon and I went to Capital Grille that night for a special dinner. He pulled out my chair for me to be seated. I went all out. I usually only wear lipstick but tonight was special. I got a Brazilian wax and my makeup done. I didn't even have to leave the house they came right to me. I haven't talked to my friends that much because all they do is ask about Brandon. In time when the shock wears off, I will start hanging with my friends again. I still can't get over Stacey calling Brandon when I was drunk. This handsome man showed up for me. He really loves to me, I thought.

"Brandon tell me about the test."

"I watched Brandon's gorgeous lips move a mile a minute. It didn't matter what he said. I'm just happy he is mine. I can't believe that I have a boyfriend. I never thought this day would come. Tonight I'm going to drink a few bottles of champagne while we are at the hotel and make love to my man.

"We have one special place to go before we go to the hotel," he said. About fifteen minutes later we arrived in front of Emack and Bolio's Ice Cream Shop where we first met. Brandon opened the Porsche door for me. We entered the ice cream shop hand and hand.

"Hey Brandon and Zoey! My two favorite people," exclaimed Fred.

"Hello Fred," Brandon and I said.

"Brandon you picked a keeper. It's nice that she comes in every week to pick up a pint ice cream for you," confirmed Fred.

"Yeah she is most definitely a keeper," he said looking down at me.

"I just wanted to stop by since I hadn't been around. I also wanted to share a moment with Zoey in the place we met."

"No problem! Good to see you," said Fred.

Brandon invited me to sit at the table where we had our first conversation.

"Who knew we would make it this far," I stated.

"I did!" said Brandon.

We sat there for a little bit holding hands and staring at each other.

"Brandon I'm ready for dessert and I'm not talking about ice cream," I said smiling.

"Well then, we better be on our way."

Dinner was amazing. Visiting the place where we first met was special. We arrived at the hotel around 8 p.m. When we entered the hotel room I stood with my back against the door pulling Brandon close. I looked up into his beautiful grey eyes that looked right through my soul. I brushed a curl from his forehead, then looked down at his expensive suit. I begin unbuttoning his dress shirt. Brandon rubbed my arms as he leaned down to kiss my lips. I desperately moved faster finally unbuttoning the last button on his shirt. Brandon turned me around so he could unzip my canary yellow dress. I turned around to look at Brandon's face. He salivated while he looked over my rhinestone bra and panties. His eyes dropped to the front of my panties that read "Brandon's."

"Looks like we understand each other," he smirked.

"Baby, can you open a bottle of Champagne?" I asked.

"Yes."

Brandon moved through the room dressed in only his slacks. I loved how we could be so comfortable around each other. Most days we walk around the house in just our underwear other times completely naked. Some days when I would drop Brandon off at the hospital I would come back in the middle of the day. I just had to see him in action. So secretly a couple of times a week I would watch Brandon with his patients. He's an amazing man. Brandon popped the top on the Champagne and poured us each a glass.

"I would like to toast to Dr. Asher, may you continue to be the best doctor you can be to your patients!"

"Thank you baby," said Brandon.

I gulped down my champagne. "Another glass please? I plan on being a very naughty girl tonight." I said unbuckling his pants.

Brandon gulped down his second glass of champagne. We set our empty glasses down on the table.

"Brandon can we look out the window and just admire the view?"

"Sure Zoey."

I stood in Brandon's arms resting my head against his bare chest. This is how we like to relax, barely wearing a stitch of clothes, enjoying each other's company.

"My friends would always joke and tell me how I broke the mold at being alone. I would live life, just not the way people thought I should live it."

"How was that working out?" asked Brandon.

"Great! My friends knew my views, accepted them, and didn't try to change me. Well, at first they did. I told them don't make any mention of me being in a relationship or we wouldn't remain friends. They respected me. Shit, of course they did, I was a load of fun." I laughed.

Brandon took my hand and led me over to the couch. I sat on my knees and continued with my story.

"Guys would always hit on me, try to date me, but I managed to get out of it. I would say I'm focusing on my studies, or my favorite line, I have a boyfriend."

"You didn't tell me you had a boyfriend."

"Brandon trust me when I say I didn't see it coming with you. Not to mention you're very smooth. You're down right pushy! The trick with the cell, putting your phone number in there, and forcing me to look at your face on my way home. I admit I was curious. I could tell the way you kissed me you wanted more and that scared me and intrigued me all at once. I put in my mind that I was going to get the sex I wanted. That kiss told me you're not a selfish lover. I figured maybe, just maybe, I would be able to get the orgasm I so desperately needed. I planned to fuck your brains out. Nevertheless, you turned the tables on me. Telling me you wanted to get to know all my cum faces really fucked me up. I wanted to be pleased so bad that I let go. I never planned on letting my walls down. Me have a man? That was farfetched because that meant I would have to tell you my deepest darkest secret that could end us."

"Zoey no it can't!" he said grabbing my face forcing me to look into his eyes. "Baby I don't give a fuck how fucked up it is, trust me I will be right here. I promise."

I cried into Brandon's arms. "Sometimes I walk past the park close to my apartment and watch the kids play. They were so cute. I walked away from the park and turned those maternal feelings off. I knew there was no beautiful house with the white picket fence and kids playing in the yard in my future."

"Baby yes there is," he said pulling my lips into his.

"Hey we are supposed to be celebrating me becoming a doctor," he said standing up taking me over his shoulder and smacking my ass.

He threw me in the middle of the oversized bed. "Zoey Robinson will become Zoey Asher," he said taking off my black and yellow bottom stilettos.

Brandon walked away for just a minute and returned with the champagne and his phone.

He sat the bottle down then stood over me with the camera phone. He snapped a picture of me in my special Brandon lingerie. He threw his phone on the chair, stood at the foot of the bed and removed my panties.

"Let me see it," he said pulling my legs apart. "Damn that pussy is pretty."

I giggled.

"Move to the top of the bed."

I did as I was told grabbing the champagne, drinking from the bottle. Brandon dropped his boxers to the floor, crawled up on the bed, taking the champagne from my hand and downing it.

"Take off your bra."

I took it off and threw it across the room. He poured champagne on breasts down my stomach, handing the bottle back to me. I set the bottle on the nightstand and watched him lick the champagne from my breasts down to my stomach.

"You taste good. Am I allowed to eat your pussy tonight or will it cause another episode?"

"No, I am going to keep my eyes open and watch you please me. No matter how good it feels I won't close my eyes. I want to cum as many times as I can tonight.

"Good."

Brandon laid on top of me, and pushed his tongue into my mouth. We both reveled in the taste of champagne on each other's breath. He circled his tongue on my neck making my pussy wet. He sucked on the tip of my chin then licked a path down between my breasts straight down to my center. Damn it felt amazing. Brandon traced his tongue along my asshole driving me insane. I gripped his shoulders tight as he licked up and down my slit. "Brandon!" I shouted as he drove his tongue into my center. "Goddamn it, Brandon!"

I watched as his head moved in a circle while he moaned.

"Baby your pussy taste so good," he said sucking up my juices.

"Oh, yeah baby, your tongue feels so good."

He woke up all my senses when he moved his flat tongue from the base of my pussy to my clit. Brandon circled his tongue repeatedly around my clit, forcing my body to jerk back and my eyes to roll back in my head. Brandon wrapped his arms around my thighs and continued to suck on my clit until he pushed me over the edge. I bit down on my bottom lip, caressed my breasts then ran my hands through his hair. I pulled him even closer to my pussy if that was at all possible. I bucked my hips driving his tongue into my center repeatedly until I came again hard. "Brandon!" I screamed.

Brandon came up for air, hovered over me, looked into my eyes, and ran his hand over his wet beard. I plunged my lips into his. I released him and ran my hands over his brown beard.

"You're gifted. Thank God you're my man."

I covered my mouth. "Don't do that baby," he said moving my hand.

"You're my woman."

Brandon held my right leg close to his body as he made love to me.

"Brandon make love to me from behind," I demanded.

He flipped me over, pulled my ass up, and then pushed in and out of me with one stroke. I met his rhythm and pushed back against him again and again. Brandon leaned down on top of me kissing my shoulder, ear, and then my lips.

"Brandon I love you," I called out as my body started to convulse.

Brandon knelt behind me, pulling me by my hips as he slammed into me.

"Whose pussy is it baby? Who's?!"

"It's yours Brandon!" I screamed as my body went limp, he slammed into me the final time, cumming inside me. I lost count of how many times I came. My pussy muscles tightened around his dick as I came again.

Brandon dropped down to my side pulling me close. He played with my ring. "You are my everything Zoey."

"I'm not done yet. You have to give me some more of my dick!" I said easing down his shaft.

Brandon chuckled.

"Sit up I want to be close to you. Brandon, I'm yours." I pulled his lips into mine, held onto his shoulders to push myself up and down his huge dick. I began moving my ass in circles to drive him insane. Brandon kissed my neck and squeezed my breasts. I turned around doing the reverse cowgirl. Brandon rubbed my back.

"Baby you feel so good shit. I'm cumming!" he groaned.

I slid up and down his dick as he exploded inside me. I laid on Brandon chest, kissed his neck, and then circled my fingertips around one of his nipples. Brandon rubbed my ass. "Zoey this is what I want forever. Us."

I looked into his grey eyes. "I'm ready to tell you my deepest secret."

"I'll be back," I stated with sad eyes. I stood to my feet and wrapped my hair in a bun. I stepped into the shower letting the water beat against my back. My Adonis of a man stood on the other side of the shower door.

"Sweetheart can I come in?"

"Yes," I replied.

He opened the shower door and I collapsed in his arms. Brandon pulled me down to the floor kissing my forehead. "It's ok," he whispered.

He caressed my frizzy hair.

"Brandon I was molested when I was fifteen by my stepfather."

I couldn't look at Brandon.

"I'm sorry that happened to you baby. I'm here for you," he said kissing my forehead and rocking me in his arms.

BRANDON

Zoey fell asleep in my arms in the shower. I wrapped a towel around her and laid her in the bed.

I watched her sleep for just a moment while I stood there soaking wet. I strolled back to the bathroom to dry off. I retrieved my cell from the couch while I threw on a clean pair of boxers. I made myself a stiff drink. I am trying to process what my woman just told me. I stood by the window, waiting patiently while the phone rings, and took another sip of my drink.

"Hello!"

"Hey little cousin!"

"Three years don't make that big a deal," I scuffed.

"Are you still coming to my graduation?"

"Of course! Shit you're graduating from Harvard as a doctor. I'm proud of you!"

"What's going on?"

"I know I don't call often, but I needed to talk to you. I can't talk to my sister about this."

"What's up?"

"My girlfriend Zoey just told me she was sexually molested when she was fifteen. I am fucking pissed! I want to kill that son of a bitch for fucking up her life."

"Do you know anything about him?"

"No she just told me, so I haven't gotten a chance to look him up."

"I plan on marrying Zoey, and I tell you this, if I ever see him I will-"

"Hey let's not be rash. I have an idea! We can discuss this matter at your graduation party."

"Sounds like a plan! See you then," I said.

I placed my cell on the table, swallowed down the last bit of scotch, and dropped my boxers to the floor. I pulled the sheet over Zoey and me. I laid on top of her kissing her neck. "Baby I need you," I whispered.

My sexual appetite for Zoey can sometimes be a bit much. Maybe I should let up a bit, I thought as plunged into her pussy.

"Umm," she whimpered.

"I Love you baby. Zoey I'm here. I'm not going anywhere. I pushed my tongue past her lips, filling her mouth with the taste of scotch. She wrapped her arms around my neck and moved her hips to meet my rhythm.

"Brandon, I'm cumming!"

"Baby, I want you to know nothing is going to change," I said as I looked into her eyes.

"You will still be my wife."

I placed both her legs on my shoulders moving a little slower until I came. That night I held Zoey tightly in my arms never wanting to let her go.

CHAPTER SEVENTEEN

GRADUATION

ZOEY

I sat with Brandon's parents and sister during the graduation ceremony. His sister was very nice.

"Zoey, we just have to do some girl outings while I'm in town," Brandon's sister Brenda insisted.

Brenda lives in New York, she also followed the family tradition and is a neurosurgeon.

Brandon looked so distinguished as he walked across the stage to the podium to make his speech. Brandon had no problem talking in front of an auditorium full of people after the ceremony. Brandon does just what he said he would do, told everyone I'm his girlfriend. Brandon didn't care who saw him kiss me. He doted over me whenever he could.

Later that night on our way to his graduation party, Brandon kept telling me how beautiful I looked. I was wearing a coral gown, bodice at the top and flowing at the bottom with a strap on one shoulder. We had a chauffeur tonight. That way we could drink as much as we wanted.

"Baby, I don't want to go to the party," he said rolling up the partition.

"Brandon don't even think about it."

"Zoey don't sit all the way over there, come here," he said pulling me close.

He held me by my waist while kissing my neck.

"Uh,uh," I whimpered.

When he rolled his tongue on my neck, I kind of lost all control. Brandon ran his hand up my dress into my panties. He slid his finger inside me, pushed it in and out, making me wet. He pulled his finger out of me and licked my juices off. He snatched my panties off and threw them on the seat next to us.

"Zoey come here I need to be inside you."

Oh yeah, I couldn't believe after telling Brandon what happened to me, everything was the same, nothing changed. What a big relief. He unbuckled his pants, pulled them down midway. Brandon helped me pull my dress up and slid me down on his dick. I watched his face as his dick filled my insides. He looked like he was already in ecstasy.

I threw my head back. The sounds my pussy made as he circled his dick inside me again and again was driving us both insane.

"I love the way you feel baby! Give me that pussy," he groaned against my chin.

I did just that. I laid my hands upon his shoulders as I moved up and down on his dick so good he was sure to cum quick. However, not Brandon, I don't know where he goes in his head but he wouldn't dare do that, and I loved that about him. Brandon held my ass tight, thrust inside me fast repeatedly until I came. I swear I saw stars as I pushed my tongue into his mouth. I felt the car stop.

"Shit Brandon, are we here?" I whispered.

"Sweetheart yes, but don't panic. Let's take our time," he stated calmly.

I cleaned us up with his extra handkerchief, and placed it in my clutch. We fixed our clothes and I fixed my makeup.

"You look absolutely ravishing," he said kissing my neck.

I couldn't help but laugh. His grandparent's estate was amazing. There were hundreds of people throughout the house and backyard, servers bustled around serving hors d'oeuvres and drinks at every turn. Brandon introduced me to so many people. I'm sure I wouldn't remember who they were if I walked past them on the street. Brandon was still having a hard time keeping his hands off of me. He kept whispering in my ear how he wanted to take me into one of the many rooms and have his way with me. The problem was he and I were never alone, there was always someone coming up to us. Finally, the couple I had been dying to meet made my acquaintance.

"Zoey it is so nice to meet you. My name is Jacob Latters and this is my wife Samantha." We shook hands and said our hellos. "Brandon has told me so much about you," he said slapping him on the back.

"I need to steal Brandon away for just a moment," said Jacob.

Brandon could see the panic in my eyes. "Don't worry she's in great hands," affirmed Samantha.

The men walked off leaving Samantha and I to entertain each other.

"This party is nice right?" she asked shaking her head no. We both giggled.

She was so nice and easy to talk too.

"It would be nice if we didn't have to meet so many people," I said.

"Well Zoey, this is your new life. Meeting new people, being away from your man for long hours and then there's the haters club," she said staring at the group of women staring daggers at me with their eyes from across the room.

"Oh, those bitches!" I recited.

"Yes that is exactly what they are, jealous, feeble minded bitches," Samantha said with a certain hate in her voice.

"Work hard at ignoring them, but not. Women can be callous and manipulative. This is what happens when a woman dates a billionaire," affirmed Samantha.

We both took a sip of our champagne.

"Especially a gorgeous one. They want your head on a stick and they will stop at nothing," she said guzzling down her champagne.

"Waiter another one please?" her voice echoed through the room full of people.

"Sounds like you know a thing or two about it," I stated.

"Yes, celebrity plus gorgeous billionaire equals plenty of jealous women. Just stay grounded, always remember he sought you out not any of them. If he didn't, we wouldn't be enjoying each other's company," she snickered.

I love Samantha already.

"Do you think it's worse because we are black women?" I asked.

"Sweetheart, that goes without saying. We are the experiment!" she stated.

"That's what one of them said to me," I said.

"They try to intimidate you because you're different. They hate their white men love our beautiful black skin. Shit, it's been like that since the beginning of time. On a lighter note your man's a doctor! That's so lifesaving!" Samantha exclaimed.

We both laughed aloud.

"I like to watch him in action. I go to the hospital and watch him work in the ER sometimes, he doesn't know I'm there."

"I love that! I can tell you love him for who he is inside. It's so touching," she confirmed hugging me.

Brandon and Jacob joined us again.

"The swirls are in the building," she stated with cheer as she raised her glass. I instantly joined her in a toast.

She's my new favorite person. We were soon separated again. A man and his wife walked over to us. The man asked Brandon several questions about his career. I flagged down a waiter for a finger sandwich. It bothered me the way Sandy stared at me, she was accompanied by three other women. Brandon's Grandfather interrupted the conversation.

"Grandfather, I would like you to meet my girlfriend Zoey."

"Call me John. Zoey it is very nice to meet you. Brandon hasn't brought a woman home in forever. The last one was Jessica. I saw her here tonight. I know if Brandon brought you here, and bought you that ring you are special," he said picking up my hand.

"It's just a piece of jewelry," I said slowly pulling my hand away.

"No, it's a promise ring," Brandon roared.

"Brandon honey," I said with my hand planted against his chest as I looked up at him.

"No, I want my Grandfather to understand I'm serious," he said looking into his grandfather's eyes.

"I truly understand and I'm happy for you Brandon."

The tension went away.

"Thanks grandfather, it means a lot."

"Brandon we will start the toast soon."

"Alright."

Jessica must have been on his heels because she walked up shortly after.

"Brandon congratulations! I'm so proud of you," she said hugging him.

"Thank you. Jessica this is my girlfriend Zoey."

"Zoey nice to meet you," she said shaking my hand.

"You look absolutely beautiful."

"Thank you. Nice to meet you, too," I said as I let her hand go.

Jessica was a chatterbox. I slipped away and Brandon didn't even notice.

I scurried to the bathroom. Upon my exit, I was greeted by Sandy and her group of mean girls.

"Come with us before we make a scene. You don't want everyone here knowing you're a tease," Sandy said angrily.

"Alright fine." My eyes meet Samantha's. I will never forget the smirk on her face.

I stepped into the study first. The women walked in behind me. One of them tried to close the door but it was pushed open by Samantha. The door swung and hit the woman in the head. I couldn't help but giggle.

"What's going on here? What possibly could the four of you want to talk to Zoey about?" asked Samantha picking up the diamond cut letter opener off the desk.

"We only want to talk to Zoey," stated Sandy.

"Well since I'm Zoey's BFF, you'll talk to us both," she affirmed playing with the letter opener.

She looked like she wanted to slit Sandy's throat.

"Francesca and I did a little digging and you will never guess what we found. You seduced your stepfather. How perverted. You see when you spewed all your shit at me; Brandon stopped talking to me. I knew I had to find some dirt on you," beseeched Sandy.

"There's nothing to share. I told Brandon I was molested. Our relationship hasn't changed, he still wants to marry me, hence the promise ring," I confirmed raising my hand.

"You fucking cunt! You think you can come here and fuck up the dynamics, well I don't think so!" Sandy spit out.

"Woo Woo," said Samantha leaping towards Sandy.

I stepped in between them and slapped Sandy across the face. "Bitch get a clue and get some standards. Brandon doesn't want you. He's made his choice, now fucking live with it."

Samantha stood against the door with the letter opener out in front ready to cut a bitch.

"You should get some self-respect. Why would you want to keep being a fuck buddy?" I asked.

"No, he was serious with me, I was coming over to his house all the time and then you entered the picture," affirmed Sandy.

"Clearly being fucked three times a month doesn't constitute a relationship. However, making love every night, telling me he could die in my pussy, and oh yeah, and again there's the promise ring," I confirmed.

"Shit that sounds damn serious," stated Samantha.

I looked at Samantha. She and I laughed.

Sandy lunged at me pushing to the floor. I jumped up and slammed her against the fireplace. I punched her in the jaw twice causing her to hit the floor. Francesca came at me next. Samantha quickly joined the fun.

"Let's play," she snarled.

Samantha punched Francesca in the jaw with a right hook then did a roundhouse kick, her stiletto met the side of her face. She was out like a light.

"We make a great team," I exclaimed to Samantha as we slapped hands.

"Becky and Sue do you want it next?" Samantha asked.

They looked at each other and ran out the room.

"Come on let's get cleaned up and rejoin the party," said Samantha.

I looked back at the women on the floor.

"Don't worry about them they will be out for a minute," confirmed Samantha.

We returned to the company of Brandon and Jacob. Everything was going great, the four of us were having the best time. I heard a woman's voice I recognized.

"Excuse me," she kept saying as she parted the crowd like the red sea.

The woman stood in front of me. She looked much older than I remembered.

"Mother!"

"Zoey."

"Brandon this is my mother Ella-,"

"What's wrong can't say my last name girl?"

"Mom not here. I would love to talk to you in private!"
"Talk about what?"

"Mother please," I pleaded not making eye contact.

"Did you tell your boyfriend how you seduced my husband? Huh?"

"Mom that's not true," I whispered.

The entire party stopped to look at us while my mother continued to make a spectacle of us."

"You are not going to come here and treat Zoey like this, I know the truth! Your husband molested her. What kind of woman takes the side of a child molester? How could you tell Zoey she's dead to you? Answer that!" beseeched Brandon.

I heard my voice over head and Maya laughing. I watched in horror. It was Maya and I at the Christmas party black mailing Martin for the concert tickets. Everyone around us watched in total shock. I heard all the 'oh my Gods and how perverted.'

I turned to my mother as I saw Sandy smirk from across the room.

"What happened to you? You once protected me. What changed?" I cried.

I marched across the room and slapped Sandy across the face. She stood there holding her face as if she was the victim. "Are you happy now? You wanted to destroy me so you could have Brandon to yourself. News flash bitch, he still doesn't want you."

I ran over to one of the maids. "Can you please open the gate?"

"Yes of course."

I pulled up my gown a bit, as I ran past all the judging looks out the front door. I thought I heard Brandon calling my name, but I couldn't be sure. I felt a tug on my shoulder. I swung my arm back and Samantha caught it.

"Come with me, my car is outside the gate."

We hopped into her Bentley.

"Where to Ma'am?"

"Just drive," said Samantha.

"Zoey where to?" asked Samantha.

"I need to go home and get some clothes so I can go back to South Carolina to be with my Grandmother," replied Zoey.

"Trevor, drive straight to the airport."

I looked out the window. Tears begin streaming down my face. Next thing I know she's talking to someone. "Jeff have the Jet fueled and ready to go, we are going to South Carolina. Be there soon, see you in a bit."

"Why are you helping me?" I asked looking over at her.

"Because I too know a little about running. He'll come after you because he loves you."

"Are you going to tell him?" I asked.

"Not if you don't want me too," said Samantha.

"I'd rather just end it here. I knew it would catch up with me."

"I know the truth but I want to hear it from you," said Samantha.

"Who's truth?" I questioned.

"Yours!" she said with piercing eyes.

"How could you possibly know?" I asked.

"I have ways of making people tell me the truth," she said pressing the button to roll up the partition.

"When you said you were molested I believed you and still do," said Samantha.

"Short version I was groomed from the age of thirteen to the age of fifteen to trust my stepfather. He told me if I wanted my mother to keep her lifestyle, I had to do something for him. He treated me like a princess. I knew it was wrong at first but I eventually got used to it. He put me on birth control showered me with gifts unt-. Until I fell in love. I became very manipulative and always got my way. That is what you saw on the screen, me getting my way.

My grandmother was in the room at the time and I didn't know it. That weekend I went to visit my grandmother and she flat out asked me. I spilled my guts like a little baby. My grandmother made sure Martin went to prison. She always told me it wasn't my fault and that my mother was wrong for disowning me. I went to live with my grandmother, I was in therapy often until I was able to deal with life again. I had no intention on being with a man seriously. I felt like I was robbed of any happiness. Nevertheless, Brandon and I met and he wouldn't back down," I smiled.

"Don't let those bitter bitches take away your happiness. You get that he isn't an average man right? He's handsome and rich. Women will always try to take him from you. But you have to stay smart and remember he only wants you," reminded Samantha.

We sat on Samantha's Jet drinking and talking about our likes and dislikes. I almost forgot about the horrible ordeal tonight. We landed in South Carolina a short time later. Samantha arranged for a car to pick me up from the airport.

"Zoey, here is some cash and don't insult me by turning it down, know that we have each other's numbers we should talk or text. Oh, one more thing, Martin corroborated your story."

"How did you talk to him?" I asked.

"Let's just say I have the muscle to make all men talk, his name is Tony. He forced the truth out of dear old Martin."

"But how did you know? I just told you tonight!"

"Brandon called Jacob expressing his fury. He just needed to vent. He never asked us to do anything, but that's what family is all about. You never have to ask, we just do. Whether you and Brandon make it, you hold a special place in my heart. We will be like sisters forever."

We laughed and hugged. "Thank God he brought you into my life. Talk to you soon."

CHAPTER EIGHTEEN

BRANDON

What a fucked up night! Shit where do I begin. Jacob pulled me into our Grandfather's study to talk.

"Jacob how's Aunt Rebecca?" I asked as I sat down on the desk.

"She's great! Listen I need to talk to you, it's important," he said standing near the fireplace.

"Brandon, I know you didn't ask for help, but I looked into Zoey's situation. I agree with you. The man needs to pay for what he did to Zoey!"

"Wait, how did you find him, I never gave you any information."

"Dude, you're a soon to be billionaire, if you think for one minute I couldn't find out her name and history, you're naive about the power of money!" he said pointing his hands to his brain.

"I sent my right hand man Tony to South Carolina correctional facility where dear old Martin Collier is housed."

"Oh, so you didn't kill him?" I asked.

"Did you want him to die?" asked Jacob.

"I don't know."

"Well this will have to do for now," Jacob said tossing a vial toward me.

"Jacob what the fuck?! You had his finger cut off? What kind of shit are you into?"

"Listen I'm a celebrity and people come after me and my family daily. I will always protect what's mine. I have a low tolerance for bullshit! Just consider it a token for the shit he did to her. Tony wanted to kill him, but I said not just yet. I wanted to speak to you first. Brandon, he groomed her since the age of thirteen to trust him and then when she was almost sixteen he had sex with her, weekend rendezvous, put her on birth control, I can go on."

I stood there like a beast my chest heaved in and out. I grabbed the edge of the desk so hard you could see the blood leave my knuckles. "When does he get out of prison?"

"In six months," confirmed Jacob.

"When he gets out I want him dead. I will be the one to carry it out."

"Do you still know how to shoot?" Jacob asked.

"Of course, all the times we went hunting together in Houston. You damn right I do."

"We can go to the range tomorrow," said Jacob.

"No need for that, grandfather has a gun range in the basement. Now tell me play by play everything that was carried out."

"I'll do you one better, I have the video," said Jacob.

After Jacob and I watched Martin get torched it made my night. I just wanted to be in Zoey's company. Everything was perfect until her mother showed up. After Zoey ran off I tore her mother a new asshole.

"You don't get to come to my family's estate spreading lies about Zoey! Your husband is a child predator who needs to stay in prison and never see the light of day. He's fucking sick! You come here all high and mighty making Zoey look and feel bad. What kind of mother doesn't stand up for her child? There is no way I would let anyone lay their hands on my child and live to talk about it. Zoey should have told you, you're dead to her."

I snapped my fingers for security. "Please remove her from the premises."

By the time I was done going off on her mom, Zoey was confronting Sandy.

"Zoey!" I called. She never looked back as she ran out of the house.

One Month Later

Today I received a package in the mail stamped from Charleston, South Carolina. My heart started racing. I opened the package and out fell the promise ring clinking against the kitchen counter. I sat here day in and day out angry with Zoey for not seeing me. She ended us because of the video that was played at my party and the bullshit with Sandy and Francesca. She said she doesn't want to deal with the women who want to be with me making her life hell. I will make Sandy and Francesca pay for what they have done. Zoey was embarrassed in front of my entire family. I think that is the real reason she doesn't want to come back. That is hard to come back from. However, we could get through it together. I had always told her that.

We never had this break up discussion in person. We had it by text message. I've been in a depressed state since she left. I don't talk to friends or family. I just keep to myself. I refuse to sit here any longer it's time for me to get Zoey back. I know you're wondering why do I want her back when she doesn't want me. I love her. She is the only woman for me.

In the days to come I watched my Zoey carry out her daily routines. She frequents the local coffee shop City Lights in her home town of Charleston, South Carolina. Every day I followed her wearing a baseball cap, sunglasses, jeans and a t-shirt. I watched her for a week and today is the first day I will make contact. Shit, get a load of this asshole. I have watched this guy flirt with Zoey every day. I want to break him in two.

"Good morning Zoey, I will get your usual. The zucchini muffin is on me," the waiter stated and winked.

I drank my coffee while watching Zoey eat her breakfast and read something on her tablet. I typed out the message on my cell phone then tapped the send button to deliver my text.

"Zoey I hope you're having a wonderful day. I bet you look beautiful."

I watched as a smile grew across her face. She placed the phone up in front of her tracing her fingers across my picture. It tore me up inside when she started crying. After she was done with her meal I followed her outside and waited for her to get into her grandmother's car. I hopped in my rental car and followed her to the grocery store. I watched her as she shopped. I sent her another text.

"I really miss seeing your face every day and watching you cook for me Zoey. Have a good day."

I watched her bite her bottom lip in confusion before I left.

My heart dropped to my feet when she replied to my text with a smiley face. I know it's not much but it's all I needed.

The next day she didn't leave the house.

I went back to my hotel room after sitting at her house most of the day.

I know you're probably thinking, why I didn't have someone else watch her since I'm rich? The answer is, I don't need anyone to watch my woman. I sat on the couch in my luxury hotel room thinking about the tons of pictures I have of Zoey. I often use a picture or my memory to beat off just about every night. I stood in the shower thinking about the way she looked in the grocery store. She was wearing a purple tank top, blue jean shorts that fit just right on her fat ass and black sandals. All that and the image of her biting her lip was enough to make me cum after I slid my hand up and down my shaft.

"Zoey," I groaned out under the shower water. I turned off the water, leapt out the shower and wrapped a towel around my waist. I sat on the bed preparing myself to make a video. My hair and chest was dripping wet.

Video message:

"Sweetheart I didn't go on my trip. I've been a basket case without you. I tried doing things your way but that's done. I want you home with me. I love you, nothing has changed. If you would have talked to me, you would have known that. Please Zoey baby talk to me."

I sent the message, dried off and went to bed.

∞

The next day Zoey returned to her normal routine. I sat in the corner with my laptop open, which I had grown accustom to doing. Zoey scanned the restaurant. "Shit!" I mumbled. She knows I'm here." I thought pulling my hat down to hide my face.

"Meet me at the fair tonight at 6:30."

I watched her stride toward the door of the coffee shop. I slouched down in my seat then cheered up at the thought of finally being able to be in her presence. I finished my breakfast than walked down the street back to my hotel. I have to admit I love the fresh air. You can smell the trees here in Charleston. The sun touching my skin feels great. I think I will drive down to Myrtle Beach later this morning. As I approached my hotel room there was someone waiting outside my door. The closer I got, I realized it was Zoey.

"So how did you know I was here let alone where I was staying?" I asked.

"I guessed. The video message you sent last night, the surroundings looked like a hotel room. I called my friend last night who works the front desk. I gave her your name and asked were you staying here. Remember I did grow up here and just about everyone knows everyone."

I watched her lips move. She batted her pretty brown eyes. Shit I wanted to be inside of her now.

"Come in," I said as I opened the door.

When she walked past me, I could smell her rose scented shampoo.

"I'm just here to talk," she said breaking away from my gaze.

I could literally make love to her for days.

"Why did you ask me to meet you at the fair?"

"To get you to stop following me," Zoey admitted.

Zoey took a seat on the couch. I sat in a chair across from her. We rehashed all the shit that happened the night she left me.

I leaned forward in my seat. "Baby, if you would have just given me a chance you would have known that I knew all I needed to know and I trusted you."

I walked over and sat next to Zoey. I pulled her chin up for our eyes to meet.

"Zoey it's just us. Do you still love me?"

A tear fell from her eye, "Yes," she whispered.

I swept her up into my arms and carried her to the bed. I removed her sandals then rubbed each of her feet. Zoey stopped me then kneeled to pull my shirt over my head. I caressed her body while she caressed my face.

"Baby I want to kill him for what he did to you," I said dropping my head against hers.

"Brandon, I was wrong for being apart from you, but I was scared of what you must have thought of me."

"Baby," I said.

"Brandon hear me out. I was that girl you saw on the video. I learned to be manipulative and I was acting out because I could and thought I loved him," she said dropping her head.

"But I'm not that girl anymore. The years of therapy helped me. Although I still didn't think I deserved love. I knew I didn't deserve you," she said laying her head against my chest.

"Baby did you want to just lay dow-." Zoey placed her hands on my face and slammed her lips against mines.

"Shit, I need you Zoey."

"Brandon I need you now and forever."

We finished peeling our clothes off each other. I laid my woman down on the bed and took my time with her. I wanted to caress every inch of her body. I laid against her body plunging my tongue into her mouth for our tongues to meet again. I sucked on her ear down to her neck, then sat up on my knees so she could see how much my dick wanted to be inside her. I lay down behind her massaging her pussy, she moaned into my mouth.

"You ready for me baby?" I asked.

"Yes." she murmured.

I slid my dick inside her, caressing her breasts, thrusting back and forth slowly.

I placed my thumb in her mouth, while I made love to her.

She sucked my thumb then screamed out. "Ah, ah, fuck, you feel so good! Brandon, I missed you, oh shit, um, I'm cumming!"

I whispered in her ear, "Come all over my dick baby. I miss this pussy Zoey. Whose is it?"

"It's yours!" she shouted as her body shook. I didn't wait for her to recover. I moved down her leg and licked up all her juices while I waited for her to cum in my mouth again. I circled my tongue around her clit until the flood gates released in my mouth. I sucked on each of her thighs then pulled her legs apart and slammed my dick into her.

This is the only woman who ever had me by the balls.

"Zoey, give it to me baby."

Zoey watched me while rubbing her breast. I hovered over her bringing her lips into mine as I thrust inside her back and forth until I came. Shit, I was so exhausted I laid down pulling her into my arms. I was so relieved to have my woman back.

∞

Later that night I watched her run around making sure the fair was a success.

The next day I met her grandmother. It was such a treat to sit down for dinner and hear stories about Zoey. While Zoey cleaned up after dinner, I took that time to talk to her Grandmother.

"Mrs. Thompson I would like to thank you for having me over for dinner. Since Zoey's father has passed away I would like to ask you for Zoey's hand in marriage?"

"Brandon do you truly understand how tough of a road Zoey has in front of her?"

"Yes," I assured her.

"When Zoey first arrived a month ago she slept off and on for about two weeks. She was extremely distraught after the garbage my daughter pulled coming to your party like that to embarrass Zoey. She rarely came out of her room. Thankfully the video chats with her psychiatrist helped. She's gotten back into a normal routine. I need you to understand she has to have a normal routine. Meaning there is something she has to do almost every day to give her balance. She goes for a run almost every day."

"Yes she does that just about every morning at home, too," I replied.

"It does appear that you actually love her. I see how you look at her. It's special. Yes, I give you my blessing to marry Zoey."

I hopped up and hugged her grandmother. The following day Zoey and I did our own thing. We went on a date at the fairgrounds. We rode the rides, played games, and took pictures. I love making a lifetime of memories with this fun and loving woman.

I took Zoey up to the tower where the judges sit during the pie eating contest. Although simple I knew what I was about to do would be memorable. Once we arrived at the top of the tower, the floodlights shined down on us. I picked up the microphone.

"Brandon what are you doing?" asked Zoey eyes wide.

I looked out at the crowd. "May I have everyone's attention please? May I have your attention?"

Several people stopped on the Fairgrounds to listen to me.

"I want to share a very special moment with you all tonight. I have been in your town for a short time and have truly enjoyed myself. I came here with the sole purpose of getting my woman back." I turned to look at Zoey.

"Zoey you make me the happiest man on this planet! You are a breath of fresh air. I was hoping to meet my special woman sooner rather than later and I definitely accomplished that," I said sniffling as a tear rolled down my face. I looked into Zoey's tearful eyes.

"This beautiful woman thought she didn't deserve to be loved," I said as I choked up trying to hold back even more tears.

"But I'm here to tell you, if anyone deserves to be loved it is this woman." I bent down on one knee, pulled the ring box from my pocket, and opened it.

"Zoey Robinson, will you marry me?"

There was dead silence.

Zoey then pulled the microphone close to her mouth and answered, "Yes!"

The crowd erupted with explosive clapping and cheers. I slid the ring on her finger then, it was as if I had tunnel vision. I didn't hear anything but the beat of my own heart. I pulled my woman into my arms, placed my lips upon hers, slowly pulling in her lips again and again.

Once we returned home to Boston, we planned to go on our trip to London for the remainder of the summer.

"Zoey, I'm going to run to the hospital to complete some paper work for my new job!" I exclaimed hugging her then smacking her on the ass.

"Umm, you naughty boy!" she moaned biting my earlobe.

"Zoey, you better stop before I make love to you a third time this morning."

"As good as it sounds we can make love again when we get to London," she said kissing my neck. "I better go for my run. I will see you when you get back," she replied pulling her arms from around my neck kissing my lips goodbye.

Zoey scurried out the door. I drove my Range Rover out of the garage on to the busy street. Traffic was at a standstill. It wasn't completely unusual, it was rush hour. I sat there for a little while, until I saw two guys standing outside their cars talking. I rolled down my window.

"Excuse me what's going on up there?" I asked.

"Someone was hit by a car," said one of the men.

"Ok, well I'm a doctor let me run and check it out," I said.

I called 911 while I walked towards the accident. "Yes I need an ambulance to the corner of Charles St. and Stuart. My name is Dr. Asher from Massachusetts General. I will let you know the status of the injured in just a sec-. "Noooooooooooo!" I screamed grabbing my head.

I dropped to my knees beside her lifeless body. She was lying on her side. I wanted to take her into my arms, but my medical training told me different.

"Zoey, honey, can you hear me?"

My hands were shaking. Not the hands of a doctor. I checked her pulse. I remembered I had dispatch on the line. "I have an African American woman petite build, concussion to the head, with a weak pulse. How far out is the ambulance?"

"Two minutes out Dr. Asher."

"Ok, thank you, good bye."

I sat the phone down. "Zoey please don't leave me," I cried.

"God I just got her back please don't take her from me," I pleaded.

The paramedics arrived at the scene. The two paramedics and I work at the same hospital. They ran over carrying an empty stretcher.

"Dr. Asher!" stated Craig the paramedic. "What happened?"

"Zoey was hit by a car."

"Dr. Asher let's get her to the hospital," said Craig placing his hand on my shoulder.

"Yeah," I responded still in shock.

I stared at the ground for a moment. There was so much blood.

"Dr. Asher we are ready to move her out."

As soon as we got into the ambulance, Zoey went into cardiac arrest. Craig rubbed the paddles together.

"Clear."

He placed the paddles on her chest trying to bring her back to life. I couldn't just sit and watch I had to help.

I watched for her vitals on the monitor. "We've got a pulse."

"Great work Dr. Asher! We will arrive at Mass General in five minutes."

"Thanks Craig". I held Zoey's hand and whispered in her ear, "It's me baby. I love you. Please stay with me, we have our whole lives ahead of us". She squeezed my hand. "Baby it's going to be ok."

When we arrived in the ER, I watched in sheer horror as Zoey stopped breathing a second time, going back into cardiac arrest.

"Dr. Asher I need you to step out!" commanded Nurse Jackie.

"I need to be in there with her," I demanded as she tried pushing me back.

"Doctor you know the routine, you can't be in here!"

Dr. Peterson is running down the hall towards me.

"Great, Charles, I need you to take care of Zoey she keeps going into cardiac arrest!" I stressed.

"Brandon, I will do everything I can. I will be right back."

I retrieved my cell from my pocket to make a call.

"Hello may I speak to Mrs. Thompson?"

"This is she."

"Hi this is Brandon, Zoey's fiancé.

"How are you?"

"I wish I was calling under different circumstances. Zoey was hit by a car and is severely injured. I am asking for your consent for Dr. Peterson to operate on Zoey. She has internal bleeding. Dr. Peterson is one of the best Trauma surgeons in the country."

"Alright you have my consent."

"Good I am sending a car service to pick you up. They will get you here in close to three hours."

"Brandon, see you soon."

"See you soon."

I called a company that specializes in catering to the rich. They will make sure Mrs. Thompson gets here on a private Jet in three hours. I paced the floor waiting for Dr. Peterson to return.

"Brandon she is still unconscious, but I have managed to keep her heart from stopping. I need to operate. We need to stop the internal bleeding. Where's her family?

"Her grandmother is flying in from South Carolina she gave consent. She doesn't get in for three hours."

"Brandon for you I will do this, anyone else no."

"Thanks Charles!"

I was going out of my mind. I wasn't supposed to watch from the doctor's galley but I didn't give a shit. Since I couldn't operate on her, myself I had to watch. I had one of the best doctors in the country doing her surgery.

I met Dr. Peterson in the hall after the surgery. "How did it go?"

"I'm going to be honest Brandon, I did everything I could. She injured her spine. Right now she does not have feeling in her legs. She will walk again. The Physical Therapy is going to be grueling. Right now she's in a medically induced coma to bring the swelling down off the brain. All we can do is wait and pray."

"Thank you," I said.

"Dr. Asher you can go in and be with Ms. Robinson."

"Thank you Jackie."

I grabbed her chart off the door before entering her room. I set the chart on the nightstand. It was pretty hard to sit there and Zoey not be able to smile back. She had several tubes running out of her body. I held her hand in mine, laid my head upon our hands and cried. I know I was supposed to be strong. The pain in my heart was too great.

~

Every day I sat there talking to her. I don't know if she could hear me, but I hoped she could. Her Grandmother and I took turns with Zoey. This allowed me the chance to go home, get cleaned up, and rest. I didn't stay away long, I would be right back at the hospital.

One afternoon my parents came to visit. They often sat with Zoey and me.

Today was different.

"Brandon can I talk to you for a minute?" my father asked walking towards the door.

"Yes," I replied following him into the hall.

"Brandon, Chip, head of the Residency department called me. He wants to know are you joining the team September 8th?"

"Dad," I sighed running my hands through my hair. "I can't leave Zoey, so if I have to give up my residency, then so be it. I will apply somewhere else later in the year."

"But Brandon this is your dream. You always wanted to work right here," my dad stated looking perplexed.

I walked closer to my father. "Are you telling me if the love of your life was fighting for her life you would leave her?"

"Son, you're being rash!"

"No she's my fiancée and there's not a chance in hell I'm leaving her side!" I spewed in fury as I rushed back into Zoey's room sitting at her bedside.

It's been a month since Dr. Peterson brought Zoey out of the medically induced coma. She's breathing on her own but she is in a deep dream state.

September 8th has come and gone. Somehow my father and grandfather pulled some strings so I can do my residency when I'm ready. I guess it pays to come from a long line of doctors. I did our normal routines, I worked all her muscles every morning and every night. I kissed Zoey's forehead then I stared at her.

"Zoey why are you giving up? I fight for you every day. When are you going to fight for yourself?"

Tonight was no different than any other except this time instead of turning on Sports I turned on Zoey's favorite reality show. After a while I fell asleep holding Zoey's hand. I later awoke to what felt like someone lightly running their hand over my head. I sat up to see Zoey's comforting brown eyes staring back at me.

"Baby you're awake!" I exclaimed.

I ran to the nurse's station. "Page Dr. Peterson, Zoey's awake!"

"Right away Dr. Asher."

When I walked back into the room Zoey was sobbing. "Zoey what happened?" I asked rushing to her side.

"I can't feel my legs," she cried.

SANDY

I've been calling the hospital posing as Zoey's mother asking about her condition. Today I called and they told me she was awake. I had to come down to the hospital and see for myself. Shit, why won't this Bitch die! I ran her down with a stolen truck. I was sure she was dead.

After Brandon's graduation party, I was sure that bitch was gone for good, but brokenhearted Brandon had to go run after her and bring her back to Boston. I recently ran into Stan who told me he was getting ready to go to London with Ted, Brandon, and Zoey. He told me when they were leaving which gave me enough time to set my plan in motion. I watched Zoey run every day for almost a week. I wanted to run her down right before their precious trip. That scanky little black bitch had to die for coming into our lives. I had Brandon first and I will be damned if she gets to keep him. I stand here at the nurses' station talking to Jackie looking through Zoey's hospital room window. Brandon is fawning all over her. I will get rid of that Bitch for good!

THE END

A Note from Shantee' A. Parks

Thank you so much for reading Samantha Posey Love Conquers. If you enjoyed it, please take a moment to leave a review.

I would be excited to hear from readers. At my website you can contact me, sign up for my newsletter to be notified of new releases, read my blog, and find me on social media.

Email poseyparkspublishing@gmail.com

www.facebook.com/PoseyParksPublishing

Twitter @posey1parks

Instagram/poseyparkspublishing

Also want more Samantha Posey and Jacob Latters visit website:

PoseyParksPublishing.com

Other Books

Samantha Posey Love Unfolded

Samantha Posey Love Reveals

Samantha Posey Love Conquers

If you enjoyed the book, please leave a review.

Thank you

Made in the USA
Charleston, SC
13 December 2016